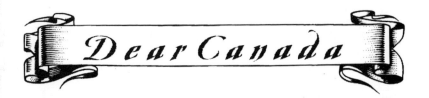

Hoping for Home

Stories of Arrival

Scholastic Canada Ltd.

Introduction copyright © 2011 by Scholastic Canada Ltd. All rights reserved. The stories in this book are the copyrighted property of their respective authors. See page 247 for continuation of copyright information.

Published by Scholastic Canada Ltd.
SCHOLASTIC and DEAR CANADA and logos are trademarks and/or registered trademarks of Scholastic Inc.

Library and Archives Canada Cataloguing in Publication

Hoping for home : stories of arrival /
Lillian Boraks-Nemetz ... [et al.] ; illustrations by Greg Ruhl.

(Dear Canada)
ISBN 978-0-545-98697-7

1. Immigrant children--Canada--Juvenile fiction. 2. Immigrants--
Canada--Juvenile fiction. 3. Children's stories, Canadian (English).
I. Boraks-Nemetz, Lillian, 1933- II. Ruhl, Greg III. Title. IV. Series:
Dear Canada

PS8323.I46H66 2011   jC813'.0108355   C2010-906018-0

No part of this publication may be reproduced or stored in a retrieval system, or transmitted in any form or by any means, electronic, mechanical, recording, or otherwise, without written permission of the publisher, Scholastic Canada Ltd., 604 King Street West, Toronto, Ontario M5V 1E1, Canada. In the case of photocopying or other reprographic copying, a licence must be obtained from Access Copyright (Canadian Copyright Licensing Agency), 1 Yonge Street, Suite 800, Toronto, Ontario M5E 1E5 (1-800-893-5777).

6 5 4 3 2 1   Printed in Canada   114   11 12 13 14 15

The display type was set in Didot.
The text was set in Goudy Old Style and Cheltenham.

First printing January 2011

Table of Contents

*For all who have forged
a home in Canada*

Introduction

Canada is a land of arrivals. For centuries, people have come to our shores hoping for freedom, or a better life, or a more promising future for their families. Immigrants from around the world have sailed here, trekked here, risked their lives to reach this land they hoped would be better, safer, more welcoming than the one they left behind. Most crossed the Atlantic or the Pacific and first set foot in Canada at ports like Halifax, Quebec City, Montreal, Vancouver. Some came by night along the Underground Railroad.

In this anthology, we have war guests and home children and refugees seeking shelter; people of different races, nationalities and backgrounds longing for a new home. Some settle in easily. Others find unexpected challenges in this new land — more hardship than they had imagined, disappointment, even discrimination. They ask questions like "Am I safe here?" "How do I fit in?" "What does it mean to be Canadian?" For a few, the arrival is not so much about place as it is about reaching a realization or a decision. But all of them wish for one thing — the promise of a future that is brighter. All are hoping, in some way, for a place to call home.

Sandra Bogart Johnston
Editor, Dear Canada Series

During World War II, hundreds of thousands of British children were sent to the countryside, away from those cities most at risk of being bombed during the Blitz. Thousands more young war guests were sent overseas through late 1939 up until the fall of 1940, to places like Canada and Australia, to keep them safe from the bombs and the fear of an invasion by Hitler.

KIT PEARSON *has written of these children before in her Guests of War Trilogy.*

Marooned in Canada

ॐ

The Diary of Verity Hall

Sault Ste. Marie to Toronto
September 1939 – August 1943

2 September 1939
Sault Ste. Marie, Ontario

We've just about finished our tour and I've forgotten to write in this journal that Dad gave me when we left England.

The truth is, I feel guilty for not doing what Dad expected me to — to record every day, so I'd always remember my first trip to Canada. He said that he wouldn't read my journal, but I know he'll ask me if I kept it up. So here's what I'll do: I'll sum up the whole trip so far, then I can tell him truthfully that I *did* write. That way I can live up to my name. Dad often reminds me that Verity means "truth." That's why I pride myself on being honest.

We've been travelling by steamer on Lake Superior, but tonight we're docked in Sault Ste. Marie. All the other girls have gone out for dinner, but I've told them I have an upset stomach. I'm lying on my bunk in the tiny room I'm sharing with Jane.

I can tell that Jane is rather fed up with me. Before she left, she suggested in her too-kind, older-sister way, that perhaps my stomach ailment is imaginary. That's because I've used this excuse before.

She is right, although I'll never admit it to her. My stomach is fine, but I'm so tired of this huge, noisy group of girls that I need an evening to myself.

Jane thinks I'm spoilt, too. She says I always get my own way, but I don't! I didn't want to come to Canada! If Jane weren't too good to be true, she'd see it my way.

Next month Jane will go to Cambridge to take medicine and become a doctor and help people. (It's hard to have a perfectly brilliant as well as a perfectly good sister.) I knew how terribly proud Mummy and Dad were of her, even before they gave her this tour of Canada as a present for all the hard work she's done.

Then they found out they had to spend all of August in France. They thought I would be bored there — I wouldn't! — so they persuaded the organizers of the tour to let me come along, even though I'm only thirteen and the rest of the girls are fifteen and up.

I tried to protest, but when Mummy sets her mind on something, one can't win. Dad understood how reluctant I was. I think that's why he gave me this journal; he thought that if I wrote down my impressions of Canada I'd appreciate it more.

I've gone off track, so I'll get back to the summary of our trip. Our party of seventy schoolgirls and six form mistresses left England in early August on the *Empress of*

Britain. We arrived in Quebec City, where everyone spoke French (but didn't understand us when we spoke the French we learned in school). Then we went on a long train journey to Montreal, Ottawa, Toronto, Winnipeg, Regina, Calgary and Vancouver, and then by ferry to Victoria. Then we came all the way back to Fort William, then we got on this steamer. I should write more about all those places, but they're such a blur.

In a few cities some of the girls gave cricket demonstrations. Jane wasn't a player, but sometimes she had to put on her school tunic and keep score. I was considered too young to play, even though I'm excellent at cricket.

The girls are from different schools all over England. No one else is from my school, of course, because it only goes up to my age. Only one girl, Imogen, is from Roedean, Jane's old school, but Jane has quickly made many friends and is very popular (of course). Some of her friends make a fuss over me, but they treat me like an infant. Two of the younger girls, Marjorie and Barbara, have tried to befriend me, but I don't care for them.

What I want is my *real* friends! Lucy and Mary and I were to spend the summer together before we all went off to boarding school: Mary to Cheltenham, and Lucy and I to Roedean. I've written them many postcards, but that makes me miss them even more.

Ever since we left England, I've had to nod and smile and tell everyone we meet how much I like Canada. I don't! Yes, the people have been immensely friendly, but the land is too vast and wild. I miss Devon's green fields and hedges, our neat villages and small shops. Canada frightens me.

I've had to stop complaining to Jane because she gets so disappointed with me. She keeps telling me to think of what I *do* like, so I'll list those things here. I like corn on the cob and maple syrup. I liked seeing cowboys on horses in Calgary. I liked some of the luxurious houses we stayed in when we stopped somewhere for a few days, and I like how everyone treats us like royalty. And I did get a great deal of pleasure from bathing in the clear Canadian lakes and paddling a canoe for the first time. One day on Lake of the Woods, when the son of our host family took Marjorie and me fishing, I caught a bass! We had it for supper and it was delicious.

There. That's as honest a summary of my trip as I can make. Everything will be fine from now on, because on Monday we go back to Toronto, then to Montreal, and then we sail home! I can't wait!

3 September 1939
Owen Sound, Ontario

A terrible thing has happened — England is at war! One of the mistresses announced it to us before breakfast. Everyone gasped and I began to cry, but Jane shushed me.

The voices around me reached such a high pitch that I couldn't bear it. As soon as we were free, Jane took me off the boat for a walk before we sailed.

We heard the sound of a radio from an open window. Jane froze and told me it was Chamberlain's voice. We listened as our prime minister announced that Britain is now at war with Germany. After I heard his voice I realized it really was the truth.

We are at war.

I clutched my stomach and told Jane I felt ill. This time I really did. Jane took me back to the boat and tucked me into my bunk. I stayed there until we reached Owen Sound.

Here is what war means: *We may not be able to go back home.*

4 September 1939
Toronto, Ontario

WE ARE MAROONED IN CANADA! We can't return to England, at least not yet. It's too dangerous to sail until a convoy can be arranged — other ships to protect our ship. That might not happen for ten days or even a *month!*

I don't remember much about the train journey from Owen Sound to Toronto. Now we're staying at the university here. I'm trying to be as brave as Jane and the others. But how can I endure being away from home for ten more days?

Later

I can hardly write this, my hand is shaking so. A few hours ago Jane came into our room. She looked so pale and frightened — frightened of what she had to tell me. My first thought was that something had happened at home, that the bombs had already started and that Mummy and Dad were dead.

Her news was almost as bad. Most of the girls will return to England in about a month, when a convoy can be found. But Jane and I will *not* return! Our parents have cabled to say that we will be safer if we stay in Canada until the war is over.

"How long?" I managed to ask.

"It's sure to be over by Christmas," Jane said. "That's what all the adults say."

"Christmas! That's four months away!" I cried. I sobbed wildly and Jane let me. She held my shoulders and to my amazement she cried a little as well. She told me how much she hated the idea of staying, how she wanted to get home and help with the war.

But then she became her impossibly perfect self. I am to be brave and sensible, to remember how I've been brought up and to behave as Mummy and Dad would expect me to.

Here is what will happen to us. Mummy has got hold of friends who live in Toronto, the Browns. They've agreed to take charge of us. Jane will live with them and attend the University of Toronto. I'll come to them on Saturdays, but the rest of the week I'm to board at a local school called Bishop something.

I protested violently, but Jane says I have no choice. Mummy thinks I should be at boarding school as planned, and that it would be too much to ask of the Browns to have me living there all the time. Jane assured me we would constantly be in touch.

I cannot believe they would do this to us. I'm sure it was all Mummy's idea — Dad would want me with him.

Jane has gone to dinner but I refuse to eat. I've cried so much my eyes are raw.

8 September 1939

I feel so numb that all I can do is write down the facts. We're now at the Browns'. Mrs. Brown came to fetch us. She's very kind and so is her husband. Their children are grown up, so they have lots of room in their large house. I have my own bedroom for when I'm not at school. They have a standard poodle called Piper who sleeps with me.

Everyone else in Toronto is as welcoming as the Browns. Our group has been taken to the "Ex" (that's the Exhibition), to see *The Wizard of Oz*, and to a reception at the lieutenant governor's.

Jane has been accepted at the University of Toronto to study science. Some of the other older girls are also attending the university. The rest are being taken in by various girls' schools here. Thirty of them will be at The Bishop Strachan School, which I will begin on Tuesday. The form mistresses who travelled with us, however, are trying to get a ship from New York so they can get back to their schools. That's so unfair! Why should *they* be allowed to go back to England and not us?

All the adults talk about is the war. A ship sailing from Britain to Canada, the *Athenia,* has been torpedoed by the Germans and many people have been drowned. Mrs. Brown says this proves how right we were not to have tried to go back, but that doesn't make me feel better. Mr. Brown thinks that soon Canada will join the war as well.

He asked us how ready England was for a war. Jane told him how we all had gas masks and many had made blackout curtains.

I hated my gas mask. It had a horrid smell and made me want to gag. A year ago we almost thought there would be a war, but then Chamberlain made a pact with Germany and everyone relaxed. After that I didn't worry about war; I just wanted to have larks with my friends. And of course Mummy and Dad would not have sent us here if they thought the war would happen. Grandfather often said there would never be a war because Hitler didn't have it in him.

How wrong we all were!

Like everyone else I am smiling and grateful, constantly thanking everyone for being so kind. Inside, I want to scream. I don't like being in a room all by myself. I clutch Piper and stare into the darkness. We haven't heard a word from home except for the cable. Are Mummy and Dad and Grandfather and Grannie and Lucy and Mary all right? Will Dad have to fight? I hate feeling so helpless.

11 September 1939

Canada has now joined the war against Germany. Everyone is still talking about the *Athenia* and waiting for news of survivors.

Since we only have the summer clothes we came with, Mrs. Brown found some old clothes of her daughter's that fit Jane, but they're too big for me. So today Mrs. Brown took me shopping. I pretended to take interest in the jerseys and skirts she bought me, but I don't care about them. She had Jane's tunics made smaller for me. I am to wear them at my new school.

12 September 1939

Here I am at BSS (that's what they call The Bishop Strachan School). It's a large stone building with a tower. So far, I dislike it intensely.

I'm the only English girl in the Middle School. There are three other girls in my room: Mollie, Kay and Sheila. We're all in Form IV-A. Mollie is the leader. Kay giggles too much and Sheila is a mouse.

They ask far too many questions and expect me to entertain them, as if I were a performing animal. Kay keeps commenting on my "lovely accent" and Sheila keeps asking me to translate different words — "jersey" instead of "sweater," or "frock" instead of "dress" — as if I spoke a different language! I answer as briefly as possible.

Now that I'm not with Jane and the Browns, I no longer feel obligated to be grateful and polite. I heard

Mollie tell Kay that I was shy and that they should be especially kind to me.

I've never been shy. I just don't wish to associate with them. They're ignorant colonial girls and I wish they would leave me alone!

The headmistress and the matron are also suffocating me with kindness. I hate feeling so obligated. None of us has any money and it's impossible for our parents to send us any. The university is paying Jane's fees; they told her it was their "war effort." Dad will have to pay back BSS after the war.

Oh, my dear old Dad, when will I hear from you?

15 September 1939

Everything is still horrid. I sleep on a narrow cot that sags in the middle. The food is appalling, except for the ice cream with maple syrup and walnuts we had on Wednesday. The classes and sports are easy enough, except they don't play netball here, they play "basketball" instead.

There are so many students compared to my little school in Exeter. We English are a motley group in our different-coloured tunics. The BSS girls don't wear tunics. They wear white middy blouses with navy collars and navy pleated skirts. Since I'm the only English girl in my class, I stand out especially in my navy tunic. I'm proud to wear it, because it's the Roedean uniform and that's where I should be instead of at a Canadian school!

I'm continuing to speak as little as possible to everyone. I don't ask questions in class and I only answer when I have to. Everyone is still unbearably kind. Jane has asked Imogen to look out for me. Jane herself has telephoned every evening, and this Saturday I'll go to the Browns' and see her again.

We had another cable from home. All it said was, *Hope you are settling in nicely, keep your spirits up.* Jane says the mail will take a long time, but I ache to hear from Dad, especially. I've already written him three long letters pleading to come home.

18 September 1939

It was a relief to have a break from prison and go to the Browns' — to eat good food and to see Jane. But she is so cheerful, it only made my mood darker. She really likes her classes and she's already made friends. I lied to her and said I had too, because I don't want her to know how aloof I've been. I could only stay until nine and next week I can't come, because the boarders are only allowed out every second week.

20 September 1939

Every day after our noon meal we have a break in our rooms before games. Today as usual the others were asking me questions about home. I will confess here that I let down my name and told them a huge lie.

I said that I was related to the Queen – that she's my mother's cousin! I made up outrageous things about going to tea at Buckingham Palace, about riding Princess Elizabeth's horse and listening to Princess Margaret playing the piano.

I couldn't stop. It was so much easier to talk about something imaginary than about my real life, which only makes me miss it more. The girls were so enthralled that we were late for games and got a detention. After games and after study I kept up the story.

Sheila, especially, follows me around and keeps asking me more questions. Mollie looks rather suspicious, but I can tell she wants to believe me.

27 September 1939

For a week the girls in my room hung on every word I said. It was as if I were a princess myself! I even had Sheila waiting on me — fetching my coat and cleaning my shoes.

Now, however, they despise me. Mollie asked Imogen if I was really related to royalty. Imogen took me for a walk and I had to confess I wasn't. She got all uppity and told me I was letting the side down, that I should jolly well shape up and tell them the truth, or else she would.

So I went back to the dorm and muttered to the girls that I'd made it all up. "Are you *sure?*" Sheila asked. How stupid she is!

Mollie and Kay looked disgusted. Mollie said, "I didn't think English girls were liars," in a cold voice.

I'm writing this as usual in the bathroom. Now no

one is speaking to me, although Sheila looks as if she wants to.

Dad would be so disappointed in me. But I seem to be a different person here. The real Verity has disappeared.

2 October 1939

We finally got letters from home. They don't help one bit. Mummy and Dad said that they were sorry we had to stay in Canada, that they missed us terribly, but that, this way, at least two members of the family would be safe. They asked us to adhere to the principles with which we have been brought up, and to settle down courageously and sensibly in our new lives. We are to remember how kind the Canadians have been to take us in and to be grateful. They hoped the war would be over soon so we could come home. They both signed the letter, but it was in Mummy's handwriting.

They aren't in any danger yet, and they have an evacuee from London living with them, a girl named Monica. Monica is sleeping in my room! A complete stranger is living in our family when I am marooned over here! Maybe my parents will start regarding her as their daughter instead of me.

I received a separate note from Dad which confirmed this. He told me how plucky Monica is, how she never cries or complains, and how he hopes that I am being as brave. He says he understands how much I want to be home, but that I am to concentrate on enjoying Canada. When I read his words I felt chilled inside. I was always Dad's pet. He called me his princess. Now he seems to prefer this Monica person.

At least Dad isn't there most of the time, so he won't spend much time with Monica. He's too old to fight, thank goodness, but he's doing secret war work in London and spends most of his time there.

When Jane showed me the letters she wouldn't let me cry. She told me I must try to be brave. I am so, so tired of hearing those words.

12 October 1939

I haven't written for a long time because there's nothing to say. Life in prison continues on its dreary way. Mollie and the others now avoid me, and I'm glad.

You wouldn't know there's a war on, except everyone still talks about the sinking of the *Athenia*. One of the BSS mistresses, Miss Hutchings, was lost, and there's going to be a memorial service for her on Sunday.

Sometimes I have bad dreams about Hitler. But surely we will beat him soon, and Jane and I can go home.

16 October 1939

This week most of the other English girls left BSS to go back to England! They finally found safe passage.

The only ones left are three Upper School girls and me. I cannot believe that my parents didn't send us on the ship. It has a convoy, so it would be safe. But they're making us stay for the duration, like cowards who are afraid to go home.

I hate my parents for doing this to me!

19 October 1939

Not only am I a liar, I have now become a bully. I can't seem to stop being cruel to Sheila. Whenever I see her thin face with its pleading brown eyes I want to shake her.

I have to record truthfully what I did, in hopes that I will stop. Yesterday morning, while we were washing, I whispered to Sheila that she'd better use lots of soap because she smelled so bad. She gasped and said, "Do I really?" Then she scrubbed her underarms so hard her skin turned red.

I told her two more times that she smelled and this morning during devotions, when we have to kneel at our beds for ten minutes while Matron inspects our rooms, I held my nose. Sheila's face turned crimson and she buried it in the counterpane.

I must stop this! Dad would be so ashamed. But I don't care. He has abandoned me in Canada and now he has another girl to be his daughter.

23 October 1939

On Saturday the Browns drove us up north to see the coloured leaves. Their splendour relieved my misery a little. Jane was so loving that I resolved to bring some of my sister's integrity back to school and to leave Sheila alone.

I only lasted one day. This morning I ragged Sheila about the costume she has chosen for the boarders' masquerade party this Friday. She was going to dress as Cinderella and I told her she should be one of the ugly stepsisters instead. She ran away from me, probably to bawl.

Why can't I stop this? At the Browns' I am in disguise as a nice person. Why can't I put on that disguise here?

Miss Lowe, the headmistress, called me into her office yesterday to ask me how I was doing. She has noticed that I'm not associating with the other girls. "I know this is a very difficult time for you," she said. She told me that if I tried to make friends here I'd find being away from home more bearable.

She's right, of course, just as Jane and my parents are right. But all the advice I hear, even from myself, just seems to roll off my back. It terrifies me what a nasty person I've become.

30 October 1939

I finally got a letter from Lucy. She adores Roedean. She told me how beautiful the school is, situated on its high cliff in Brighton. I know that, of course, from visiting Jane there.

Lucy seems to have made many new friends. She didn't say anything at all about the war. She seems perfectly safe at Roedean — as *I* would be if I were there with her! She only asked how I was at the end of the letter, and she didn't say she missed me. I haven't heard at all from Mary. Have they abandoned me as well?

1 November 1939

I've been trying to let up on Sheila, but this evening I called her "Butterfingers" when she dropped her fork at supper. Of course she dropped it again.

5 November 1939

I will write as true an account as I can of the last two days.

Yesterday was so rainy we had to climb ropes in the gymnasium instead of playing lacrosse. As we were changing for study, Mollie and Kay started talking about their fathers and what they were going to do in the war. Mollie's father is joining the Army and Kay's is joining the Air Force. They were going on and on about how much they would miss them.

I felt such a pang for Dad that I almost doubled over. I glanced at Sheila, who hadn't said a word.

"What's *your* father going to do, Sheila?" I asked her. "I bet he's too cowardly to fight, just as you would be."

Sheila ran out of the room.

Mollie yelled, "You idiot! Sheila's father is *dead!*"

Then Kay started shouting as well. They told me how awful I was, that they wished I had never come to

BSS, and that they were sick and tired of my being such an English snob.

I rushed down the stairs and out the door. No one saw me. I couldn't stop running. The rain was pelting down and I got soaked, but it felt cleansing, as if it were washing off my nastiness.

Finally I spotted a shed at the bottom of the lower playing field and I went into it. I huddled on the floor and my tears poured out faster than the rain.

How *could* I have said such a thing? What kind of monster have I turned into? I thought of poor Sheila without a father . . . at least I *had* one. Then I thought of how disappointed Dad would be if he knew how I've behaved in Canada, and I cried even harder.

I didn't have a hankie and my face was a mess. I got so cold I couldn't stop shivering, but I didn't know where to go. I wanted Jane, but I didn't know the way to the university and I didn't have any money to get there. I wanted Dad and Mummy. But all I had was myself.

Finally I stumbled across the field and back into the school; it was the only place to go. When I got in the door I could hear everyone else at supper. Matron was coming down the stairs. She was astonished to see me standing there, sopping wet and trembling. She asked where I'd been. I mumbled that I'd gone for a walk because I felt ill and didn't want to eat.

Matron was very kind. She took me up to the infirmary and tucked me into bed with a hot water bottle. She stroked my hair the same way that Mummy used to when I was small, until I fell asleep.

The next thing I knew, it was morning. I stretched out in the sunlight and felt clean and good. Matron brought me breakfast, and when I told her I was better she let me go back to my room.

It was an in-Saturday, so I knew the others would be there. I stood outside the room and listened to the jazz coming from their gramophone. Then I walked in slowly, as terrified as if I were facing Hitler.

First I told Sheila how sorry I was for what I said, and for being so cruel to her all term. Mollie glared at that, so I guess Sheila never told her. Then I apologized to the others for being so unfriendly.

They all just stared at me. I think it's going to take a while before they accept my apology. I tried to be as nice as possible to them all day, especially Sheila. After tea I invited her to go for a walk; to my relief, she accepted. Then I asked her about her father.

Her words tumbled out. He died last year of cancer. Sheila was his only daughter — she has two younger brothers. Her eyes filled with tears as she told me how he laughed at her jokes, how he called her Pixie.

Then I told her about Dad, how he called me Princess and how much I miss him. I even told her about Monica.

"He's probably being so nice to her because he misses you so much," said Sheila.

I decided to believe her.

Later

The others are asleep and I'm writing in the bathroom. After this I won't write any more.

We had such a cosy evening. All the boarders gathered in the parlour and one of the mistresses played the piano while we sang. The three other English girls and I really belted out the words to "There'll Always Be an England." I enjoyed a Canadian song called "Alouette." I was squished between Mollie and Sheila on the floor and they didn't seem to mind.

I think it will take a long time before they trust me, especially Mollie, but I am going to try my very best to win them over.

1943

8 August 1943

I found this old journal when I was packing. I immediately sat down to read it, and now I will finish the story of my time in Canada. In a few days I'll be going home! The seas are safer now. Mummy and Dad never thought I'd be in Canada for four whole years. They miss me so much that they will risk bringing me back.

Jane is staying because she got married! Her husband is a very nice boy called Peter Sutherland, a Canadian who is also studying medicine. Her wedding was very small: just myself, the Browns, and a few of Jane's and Peter's friends. It felt so odd that she was getting married without Mummy and Dad present. Now

Jane and Peter are living happily in a tiny apartment near the university. I will miss my dear sister terribly, but she and Peter will visit England as soon as they can.

The war has been long and horrendous. Last spring Exeter was bombed, but our house and the cathedral are still standing.

Monica returned home to London in 1940 because it seemed safe. At the end of the year, however, she and her parents were killed in the Blitz. That is *so* tragic. I wish I had met Monica.

My parents have warned me how changed life is in England now, with the blackout and rationing and the ravaged cities. For my last year of school I'm to board at Roedean as planned, but it has been evacuated to Keswick! Lucy says they're having a super time there. Once I've finished school, I intend to join the Wrens and do my bit to help win the war.

It was very painful to read over this journal. What a snotty little brat I was! Jane was right — I was indeed spoilt.

I don't think I am now. Perhaps being stranded ended up being good for me. After I was so cruel to Sheila, I had to take myself in hand and turn over a new leaf.

I think I've succeeded. Mollie and Kay and Sheila and I are now fast friends and I will miss them very much. I even spent July with Mollie in Edmonton — I got along well with her family, especially with Sandy, her handsome older brother! Sandy is hoping to join up and has promised to come and see me in England.

As the war got worse, many children were sent from England to safety in Canada. They were called "war guests." I suppose that's what I was too — one of the first! A few years ago there were about eighty English girls at BSS. I really enjoyed introducing Canadian customs to them.

In many ways I *am* a Canadian now. I've learnt to ski and canoe and skate, and my favourite food is still maple syrup! I've seen many parts of this beautiful country, and its vastness no longer scares me — in fact, England will probably seem small and cramped compared to it.

I am really English, of course, and I long to be home. But one day I will return to this country that took me in when I was stranded and afraid.

Amy doesn't understand why her bank manager father has been sent away to build roads. Or why her mother is so sad. Most of all, she doesn't understand why her older sister Kay is so angry. Yes, it's wartime, but Japan and Germany are far away. So why are the Japanese Canadians being rounded up and sent to live in camps in the B.C. interior? Amy can't help thinking of the trip as an adventure, but that isn't how it strikes Kay.

SHELLEY TANAKA's *family was interned in British Columbia's interior during World War II, along with thousands of other Canadians of Japanese ancestry.*

Ghost Town

ᕮ

The Diaries of Amy and Kay Yoshida

Vancouver, British Columbia
May 1942

May 2, 1942

My family is shrinking.

First Dad left. A lot of men had to go away. Mr. Oda and Mr. Sato and all the others. They have to build a new highway across B.C. The government needs workers to move rocks and clear bushes. I don't know if Dad will be very good at that.

Then after Dad left, Marie got married to Shig, and after that they moved all the way to the other side of the country, to Ontario. I thought maybe I would be the flower girl and get a puffy dress, but it wasn't a wedding like that. Marie wore a regular suit and she just carried tulips from our garden. She got a new hat though.

I didn't even go to the wedding. It was just down at city hall, not even in a church. Kay went and she came home and slammed the door. I don't know why. Now she can be the oldest and have her own room and not share with me anymore.

So now there are just three of us. And Lucky, of course, but Mother says cats are not real family members.

I think Mother misses Dad. But it's not his fault. All the men had to go. The government made them. Except ones like Uncle Bing, who is too old.

It's because there's a war on. The whites don't like Japanese people anymore. Kay says they never did, but I don't think that's right. The kids in my class used to like me. They came over in the summer and we played baseball in the empty lot across the street and Mother would come out and peel oranges for everyone. She's the best orange peeler. She even takes off the stringy white stuff.

Now those kids don't like me as much. They do this thing with their eyes, pulling the corners up and down to make them slanted. Chinese people are supposed to have eyes that slant up, and Japanese people are supposed to have eyes that slant down. The kids say "Chinese!" Pull eyes up. "Japanese!" Pull eyes down. "They had a baby!" Pull one eye up and one eye down. Then they laugh their heads off.

It's not mean exactly, but it's not nice either.

It's because the Japs bombed Pearl Harbor before Christmas, so they are getting closer. Everyone says the next stop after Hawaii is Vancouver. Billy Sinclair says in B.C. we should be more scared of the Japs than of Hitler because Japan is closer than Germany. He says the Japs have bombs that can fly all the way across the Pacific and land here.

It's a good thing Kay isn't reading this. She says don't say "Japs" because it's insulting. But it's just a short form, isn't it?

I can hear Mother crying sometimes at night. She has to lie down a lot and sometimes she is sick in the bathroom. I think maybe she is heartsick from missing Dad.

Mother says I have to help out more now, but there is not much extra to do. Dad was busy but mostly with his clubs. Tennis club and judo club and kendo club and chrysanthemum club. Lots of clubs.

The main thing I have to do is weed the beets and pole beans and look after his chrysanthemums. Mrs. Parks says Dad loves his flowers more than his three daughters. He grows them so big and perfect that they win prizes. His flowers, I mean.

I am in charge of earwigs. Here's what you do. You go out after dark. Take a flashlight and tiptoe over to the chrysanthemum bed. Turn on the light and flip up a leaf and if you see an earwig, you flick it off fast and then stomp on it!

Dad squishes them in his fingers. Ugh. He can do potato bugs like that too.

Not me. I flick them off with a stick and step on them. Sometimes they get away but at least they aren't eating the chrysanthemums anymore.

I'm going to do homework now. Normal homework like Arithmetic and English and then Japanese school homework. Sigh.

It's not fair. First I go to regular school all day and then when everyone else goes home and buys an Orange Crush at the store or maybe plays badminton, I have to go to Japanese school until 5:30. And on Saturday morning too!

Lately Mr. T. has been spending a lot of time talking about being Japanese. He says we are a special race because we have special strength. It comes from your *hara,* which is a little spot behind your belly button. But he says we are Canadian first, because we were born in Canada.

So which is it?

May 13, 1942

We are packing to leave Vancouver! The prime minister says it is just for now, to keep us safe from people who think we're bad like real Japanese people.

Who cares? No more school for me!

We are going to a town called Kaslo. It is in the Rockies, right beside a lake! I am so excited.

I am packing all my treasures. I need to take Mackenzie Bear and my parcheesi set and my diary. I also made a special box for Lucky, with a handle and a little window so he can see out.

May 16, 1942

Maybe writing it down will help. Heaven knows there's no one to talk to. Families huddled together, people pretending to sleep. The noises echoing off the roof of this old cattle barn. They've put us in livestock buildings on the exhibition grounds, crammed in like sardines, under guard until they decide what to do with us. The dust and the smell are making Mother feel even worse than usual.

Why didn't I leave when I had the chance? The evacuation has been going on for months. Why didn't I go after Auntie and Uncle had their car and their farm confiscated and were shipped off to Greenwood? After Dad and all the other able-bodied men were sent to the work camps? Dad, on a road crew! Dad, who writes haiku and tends his chrysanthemums when he's not at the bank.

But Mother just closed her eyes and her ears and pretended nothing was happening.

I knew things would only get worse. But I was hoping against hope that I could finish high school, and then go east to join Marie and Shig. I thought she was crazy getting married so fast like that, when she's been dreaming about a church wedding and a long white gown ever since we were kids. But she wanted to get out so badly, and she couldn't go on her own. I guess Shig's brother out east will help them get settled.

It was so strange going back to empty my locker after we got our notice that we had to leave Vancouver. The buzzer rang and everyone disappeared into their classrooms and then it was just me in the hallway. I never realized how wide the halls were, how quiet they could sound. The walk to the office seemed to take forever, and it didn't even seem real when they took my name off the enrolment list. And just one month away from graduation! When the principal came out and shook my hand, I wanted to scream.

How will I ever get my diploma now? What about university? What about my life?

Instead we're being evacuated to Kaslo, an old silver-mining town in the Kootenays. Mother says we're lucky, that we'll be living in real buildings instead of tents or tarpaper shacks like some of the others.

We were so stupid — that's what I realize now. What Marie must have realized when she married Shig and moved to Ontario. We thought if we behaved ourselves and stayed quiet, the government would know we weren't a threat after all. Now we've been kicked out of the homes we've lived in our entire lives. Kicked out of the cities we were *born* in.

Why not persecute the German Canadians, the Italian Canadians?

We all know why. It's because Japanese look different. We're easy to spot. Now they think getting rid of all the Japanese in Canada will solve their problems.

Prove you're Canadian by cooperating, the prime minister says. Do what you're told. Go where we tell you.

So we do.

Like sheep. We are good little sheep.

We are not in Kaslo yet. First a bus brought us to a big barn at Hastings Park. We had to line up to be organized, and we are even sleeping overnight here. There are no rooms, so we sleep in the section where cows used to be. There are just blankets for walls. People are coughing and blowing their noses everywhere and there is one lady who cries a lot.

I thought it was all right here at first, but Kay says it is disgusting and we are being treated like animals. There are bunk beds and bunches of straw that you stuff into a bag to make your own mattress. It's lumpy and the straw pokes into your back like needles. I sniffed it to see if maybe a cow had already slept on it, but it's hard to tell.

It all happened really fast. The buses came and we had to go and Mother said we couldn't take Lucky. Even though I made his special box and everything.

I cried then, but that was the only time.

The government says each person can only bring a certain amount. Just 150 pounds for grown-ups and 75 pounds for children. And we have to bring food and mattresses and blankets and even our sewing machine. So Mother said I could only bring my diary and tiny treasures like my necklace with the red stone that looks like a real ruby. I had to leave Mackenzie and all my big dolls and games behind.

I was so mad! Why a sewing machine? Kay says they want us to be able to sew our own clothes and such. She says that means we will not be coming home for a long time.

Can she be right? I don't like to think so, but usually she is.

May 17, 1942

I have a new friend. Her name is Irene.

I was in our stall at Hastings and I was feeling sad about Lucky. Our neighbours down the street said they would look after him, but I don't know. Their kitchen isn't like ours, with the warm spot behind the stove where he likes to sleep.

Cats don't like change. They like things the way they like them.

I was lying in my bunk next to the blanket between the stalls. I was listening to the coughing and sneezing and the Crying Lady, crying as usual.

Then someone stuck a note between the blankets and this is what it said.

Hello. My name is Irene. What's yours?

So I wrote a note back and now we are friends. We go up and down the stalls and look at feet under the blankets and make up funny stories about them. Some people don't even have blankets to hang for walls, and they have to use coats and skirts instead.

Irene has been here for two whole months. She says when she came they didn't even have walls around the toilets! She says living in the cow stalls is better than living in the pig section, which smells even more because cows eat grass but pigs eat anything, so their poo stinks worse.

Irene is going to Kaslo too! She lives on Vancouver Island. Her father was taken away just like Dad, and after that all the Japanese families on the island were sent here to Hastings. Irene says they wanted to get rid of all the island people first because a lot of them are fishermen. The government is afraid they might take messages out to Japanese submarines and sneak enemy soldiers into Canada in the dead of night. That's why they took their boats away, too.

Irene says the Mounties told her mother they could go home after three months, so don't bother to bring too much.

So I told her about our sewing machine and how Mother dug up all her peony plants in the garden and gave them to a lady from church.

Irene got real quiet then.

May 17, 1942

We had so little time to get ready, to decide what to take, what to leave. And there was Mother, out in the rain, digging up her peonies! Instead of organizing all our things. She thinks we can just lock our belongings in a room to keep them safe! Uncle said it will be a long time before we'll be allowed to come back and that we should leave our belongings with neighbours we trust, but Mother doesn't want people poking into our things.

I watched her digging in the rain, and that's when I saw. Her apron all wet and plastered to her stomach.

She's pregnant. That explains the morning sickness, her tiredness, her moods. Oh, I can't believe it. She's forty-two! And now we're on our way to a camp and who knows what kind of conditions.

I wonder if Marie knew and didn't tell me. If that's why she was so anxious to leave Vancouver. Marrying Shig so fast like that. Not just to avoid the camps. To get out of becoming chief nursemaid and bottle washer for Mother and a screaming infant. And babysitter for impossible Amy.

Amy. Never lends a hand, needs to be reminded to carry her own bag. She's worse than a toddler.

Look at her. Running around with her little chatter-box friend. The Gruesome Twosome. Scribbling in their diaries, writing their silly notes.

It's as if she thinks it's fun to sleep in a cattle barn. Eat bologna sandwiches in a crowded dining hall with thousands of strangers.

It's all just a game to her, a big adventure.

May 19, 1942

We're on a train now. Going to Kaslo. We had to line up and wait for a long time. It's all Japanese people here, but mostly mothers and kids and old men. I miss Dad. The Crying Lady is also on the train. Too bad.

The seats on the train are hard so Irene and I put pillowcases filled with clothes on top to make cushions. But when Kay saw she got really mad. She said inside all the clothes are fragile items like Mother's tea set, and that we will crack them.

When she yelled we jumped off our seats right away but then we looked down and we could see our bum marks on the pillows. We looked at each other and started laughing our heads off and Kay looked like she was going to slug me.

Irene says Kay is prissy and bossy and that's probably why she doesn't have a boyfriend. She says when Kay gets mad she gets two little straight black lines between her eyes. It makes her look like a witch.

So now we call her the Wicked Witch. But just behind her back.

May 20, 1942

The train trip lasted forever. Then we came to a place beside the water and we had to wait some more. But now we are on a SHIP! It is three storeys high with a cabin on top for the captain and a smokestack behind it. Roy S. says it is not a real ship. He says the *Titanic* was a ship and it had four smokestacks.

I don't care. This is fancy like a ship, even if there are a lot of us crowded on it. Some rooms have carpets and red velvet curtains.

The lake we are on is called Kootenay Lake and it is very skinny. You can stand at the railing and watch the trees and the mountains slide by on both sides. Kay came and we watched the lake together for a bit. I remembered a story she used to read me when I was little, about a boy named Momotaro who floats down a river in a giant peach and is adopted by a kind old couple who live in the mountains.

Kay said that peach could float down this lake all the way to the Columbia River, and from there all the way to the Pacific Ocean. I said could you float all the way from here to Japan and she said you could and we had a little chat about that and it was nice.

When I told Irene she said, "It's just like the Wicked Witch to turn everything into a geography lesson."

There is a poster on the ship that says we must be careful of SNEAK THIEVES. We must sleep with our valuables under our pillows, which I would do, except we didn't bring pillows.

Kay found one of my private notes to Irene and she says my handwriting is atrocious. She underlined all my spelling mistakes and wrote ATROCIOUS PEN-MANSHIP in the margin. She is cross because I have started making my *e*s like backwards *3*s, the way Irene does. I think it looks cute but Kay says *e*s should look like little loops and writing should slant forward, not go up and down.

Kay's handwriting is perfect. She has a certificate that says so from the MacLean Method of Hand-writing. She is very artistic. Even when she wraps presents or ties a hair bow it looks different. Better than when other people do it. Irene says that means she must be weak in other things but I don't know. She's a champion public speaker too and last year she won a big contest. The trophy was HUGE. Bigger than the one Dad won for his chrysanthemums. He pretended he didn't notice, but he did.

Anyway, she says my writing is not up to standard and that she would never allow it if she was the teacher.

Later

There is this boy on the ship. Maybe I have mentioned him. Roy S. His ears are quite big. Irene calls him Dumbo. He wears a cowboy hat and he says things like "man alive" and "no guff." He calls everyone "pardner" — "All right then, pard." "You got it, pard." He says "chow" instead of "food."

Roy likes to draw but he just draws the same thing over and over. Robots. He says in the future robots will do everything, like sweep the floor and mow the lawn and wash the clothes. He always talks about his dogs back on his berry farm. Grouch and Skipper.

Lots of us left our pets behind, but we don't keep talking about it.

Anyway, Roy has this box that he carries around everywhere. It looks like a regular biscuit tin but it rattles in a funny way. He has secret papers in the box, too, and a Brownie camera. We saw him take it out once and show the other boys.

Irene says he will be arrested if the Mounties find out he has a camera. Japanese aren't allowed to have cameras or radios.

We call the biscuit tin his spy kit. We are going to watch him closely.

May 20, 1942

We're on the S.S. *Nasookin*, the sternwheeler that will take us the final leg of our journey, up the lake to Kaslo. The smell of the coal-fired engine is strong and the drone of the engine and the hissing of the boilers have given me an awful headache.

Mother sits huddled in a corner feeling ill. At least she's not constantly weeping like the woman Amy calls the Crying Lady. On the other side of the saloon deck a woman is knitting socks. To send to the soldiers fighting in Europe, she says. To prove we are good Canadians in spite of what our own government is doing to us.

Some of the women are already meeting to make plans for our lives in Kaslo. We haven't even arrived and they are busy chattering away about how this is the beginning of the beginning. *Shikata-ga-nai,* they say. It can't be helped. We must make the best of things.

They're worried the children should not miss any school, that they must be kept occupied once we arrive. It seems the government is too busy moving all of us around to be bothered with things like education. There are too many children to attend the local schools, and there are no real teachers among us. So someone had the bright idea that those who have graduated high school can teach the little ones.

They have pulled me into the group, even though right now I should be at home studying for my exams and getting ready to go to UBC.

They are buzzing like bees, so excited. They're already planning concerts and excursions and activities. When we don't even have a schoolroom! No desks, no blackboards, no books.

I can't wait to see the look on Amy's face when she finds out she's not really on summer holiday after all. And that I might be her new teacher!

May 21, 1942

We're in Kaslo. Waiting. That's what I am doing now. Sitting on the dock with our suitcases and bags and boxes. Most people don't even have real suitcases. Just boxes tied together with rope, and flour sacks and pillowcases stuffed with clothes.

Mother is feeling sick again so Kay took her to find a bathroom. She says watch our things and don't dare run off with my "little friend" for even a second. She means Irene.

Now we are all just waiting for someone to tell us where to go next.

This is what Kaslo looks like. There is a bay on one side and a park and a little beach for swimming. And we passed a little creek with a bubbly waterfall coming right into the lake! Irene says she made a kingdom beside the creek behind her house and that we can do the same thing here when we find the perfect spot. I can't wait!

All around are mountains. Not real mountains like around Vancouver, but more like big hills, with trees and little patches of rock and they slide right into the lake, except for a flat part that sticks out and that's where they put Kaslo.

They call Kaslo a ghost town but there are real people already living here. I can see a girl with fluffy golden hair standing on the edge of the park. I pretend I don't see her and she is pretending not to see me too. She has a big ribbon in her curly hair. I love curly hair. When Kay was still nice she sometimes put rag curlers in my hair for me. But it was lumpy to sleep on and the next day the curl only lasted until lunchtime.

The buildings here look a little shabby but we haven't seen the hotel yet. Because that's where we are going to live. In a hotel!

I have never been in a hotel, but there is a big one in Vancouver and Irene says all the sinks have gold faucets and there are fancy chandeliers everywhere. She says her uncle stayed in a hotel in Hawaii when he came from Japan. In Hawaii hotels you can have fresh pineapple juice whenever you want and in the restaurant they fold the napkins to look like fans and there are orchids growing everywhere. Irene says orchids are the most expensive fl owers in the world, and every night when the maid comes in to turn down your sheets she puts one on your pillow. That's so you will have sweet dreams.

A little later

Something bad just happened. Roy S. was sitting with his family on the dock. He climbed up onto a pile of trunks and suitcases even though his mother told him not to. He sat up there and looked at me like he was the king of the castle.

Then he got out his spy kit. And when he tried to open it the top stuck and he yanked it and everything fell out. Robot drawings and his Brownie camera and about a million marbles. *Ai-yai-yai!* They all spilled! Rolled down and off the dock and plop into the water.

He tried to catch them and fell off the suitcases and skinned his knee. Then he cried and his mother grabbed his arm and yelled at him. "Stop that. Boys don't cry," she said. She shook him a bit when she said it.

But there is lots of crying here. The Crying Lady, for one. She never stops and she doesn't even have anything to cry about.

May 21, 1942

I'm in our new "home." It is indeed a hotel. The Langham. We have one room on the second floor. Bunk beds still smelling of fresh-cut wood. Straw mattresses. Work teams were sent ahead to make the buildings ready for our arrival. Japanese Canadian men. It's like making prisoners build their own cells.

Peeling paint and brown water spots on the ceiling. The bathroom and WC downstairs. A single window with a cracked pane. Old newspapers pasted to the walls. That must mean it gets cold here in the winter. Dead flies everywhere.

No chandelier.

I know all about the chandeliers and the ridiculous stories Irene has been telling Amy about how glamorous hotels are. How could I not know? She's such a scatter-brain. Leaves her precious diary lying about for someone else to tidy up. How could I not read it? I know what she writes about me, the Wicked Witch.

Wait until she sees our "hotel" room. That will shock the nonsense right out of her.

I'm supposed to be up here unpacking. But how can I? The room is so small. There's nowhere to put things, nowhere to hang things. I made the beds as best I could, cracked my head twice on the top bunk trying to tuck in the blanket.

Kaslo is very small, very quiet. There are a couple of churches, a grocery store. It's hard to imagine it was once a boom town, the hotels filled every night, the trains bringing boxcars of silver from the mines to the boat dock.

Mother says this is not a prison camp because we are not living in tents or barracks, and there are no fences. What a joke. The mountains at our back, the lake in front, Mounties at both ends of town guarding the single road. Who needs fences?

And I saw the locals, peeking out from behind their curtains as we walked to our assigned quarters.

We must become tough if we are to make good here, the Reverend says. Every life experience, he says, is an opportunity for the training of character. We must not forget that we still have a vast realm within which we are free to choose and decide.

An opportunity! Free to choose!

How long do they expect us to stay here, pretending to make the best of things? Until the war is over? When will that be? How can I get on with my life in this place? Stuck here with Amy and Mother, who will only become more and more helpless with this ridiculous pregnancy.

I can hear her now, downstairs with the other women. All trying to cook on the single stove. Complaining about the green wood and arguing about who will cook their pot of rice first. Their voices get higher and more shrill with each minute. I can smell rice water burning.

Later

I sat by the window for a long time. Too tired to do anymore, so I just looked out the window and watched them. The Gruesome Twosome and the other youngsters, sent out to play while the grown-ups "get settled" in their rooms. They looked like street urchins, crumpled and dirty.

But for the first time, Amy and Irene were quiet. Not chattering or giggling behind their hands. They were sitting together on an overturned washtub, looking around.

And I could tell they saw it all. The broken fence, the overgrown patches of dirt, the thistles and weeds. Garbage and building scraps everywhere.

Then the sun came out. Just broke through the clouds. And suddenly Amy and Irene jumped to their feet. And then all the children were running in the yard, leaping up and down like they had gone crazy. Laughing, waving their arms, reaching up.

I didn't understand at first. And then I saw. Fluffy cottonwood seeds, floating everywhere, somehow sparkling in the sun. And Amy and her little friends, leaping up to catch them.

Sun fairies, I heard her call them.

Beyond them I saw tiny bright orange flowers in the weed patches on the edge of the yard. Sticking up in bunches on straight stems. In the sunlight they glowed like fire.

In my suitcase I have a soft wool sweater that I can

fold and put in a pillowcase to make a pillow. Then maybe I'll go out and pick some of those orange flowers. There's a satin ribbon woven into the neckline of one of my nightgowns. Maybe I can use that to tie a little bouquet.

Maybe I'll put it on Amy's pillow.

For sweet dreams.

Zayd and his family have left Pakistan and after
a few years in England decide to move to Canada,
hoping that the racism they faced in England
won't follow them across the Atlantic. Most Asians were
not allowed to immigrate to Canada until the early 1960s.
Even in cities, their numbers were small.

When **RUKHSANA KHAN**'s *family came to Canada*
from Pakistan in 1965, they were the only Pakistani
Muslims in their small southwestern Ontario town.
Her father did choose between Canada and
the United States because he liked
the Canadian flag better.

To Get Away from All That

❧

The Diary of Zayd Hassan

Hamilton, Ontario
November 1964 – January 1965

November 19th, 1964

If it weren't for Rudyard Kipling and Mr. James, I'd be fast asleep by now, like Farkhanda is, like my parents are, like any sane person would be after such a long day. I'm exhausted after helping Abugee carry our massive trunk up seven flights of stairs to our new home, and then unpacking.

But I said I was going to start a journal the first day we arrived in our new land, and I'm doing it.

It won't be like those dusty volumes that Mr. James kept on the bookshelves behind his desk.

But I do mean to record my history, our history, as if it were just as important.

How our teachers back in Pakistan would go on and on about the glory of Britain! Like the one time Mr. James brought in a chit of paper that was ragged and torn around the edges. It didn't look impressive but he held it like it was made of gold. It was a note, addressed to him, that Rudyard Kipling had written. I got to thinking right there and then, Is that British habit of documenting everything so thoroughly what gives them some kind of advantage? Is it that they value their past experiences, instead of like so many Pakistanis I know, who live life day to day, never looking back?

I decided right then that I would try this for myself.

Why not? I'm named after Zayd bin Thabit, the Prophet's (peace be upon him) scribe. Why shouldn't I chronicle my life so that one day I can look back and see where I've been? You never know, maybe one day someone will hold up a slip of paper I once wrote upon and marvel at its value.

Ha! Imagine me becoming as famous as Rudyard Kipling!

Never mind, I might find value in keeping a journal.

When we disembarked this morning in Toronto and drove to the ragtag apartment building here on Caroline Street in Hamilton, I thought, What better time to start than on the first day we arrived here in Canada, a land both exciting and foreign, with no mango or guava trees and not a wild parrot to be seen?

There's a tiny snore coming from Farkhanda. She was fast asleep on a mattress on the other side of the room, but she rolls over, opens her eyes, sees the bare bulb shining and says, "*Bhai jehan,* why aren't you sleeping?"

"Just now. Go back to sleep."

So she turns over and does, just like that. When I

was six, I could sleep like that too. Not a care in the world.

Dadiami said that when I was born there was much rejoicing. (But the funny thing about Pakistanis and sons is that they want us more than anything, but once we're actually here we're treated pretty hard.)

When Farkhanda finally came along, there was little rejoicing. Some people wondered what Abugee had done wrong. Others reassured Amigee not to worry — the next child might be a boy. (She just rolled her eyes when they weren't looking.) Farkhanda is the pet of the family, and gets away with things I wouldn't even think of. Nothing is expected of her except to be pretty and to grow up and get married.

There never will be a next child. The doctor says Amigee can't have any more, so now all my father's hopes are pinned on me. It's a lot of pressure. Abugee decided we'd leave our large beautiful house in the warmth of Pakistan to spend three years in a one-room flat in Southall, so close to Heathrow you could hear the jets taking off even inside. With only one privy for everyone in the building, we had to put on our coat and boots to go to the toilet. Amigee was always afraid of the gangs of white teenagers who'd come around.

Abugee tried to buy us a house in a nicer neighbourhood, but when he'd answer the adverts in the paper the homeowners would say they only wanted to sell to white people, and close the door in his face.

Someone told Abugee to go to North America, so he

took me with him to the embassies because my English is better than his.

On the roof of the American embassy was a huge statue of an eagle that looked ready to pounce. The Canadian flag had a Union Jack in the corner and an ugly crest, but no pouncing eagles. We chose Canada. As soon as the laws changed a couple of years ago and Canada was allowing non-whites to come, Abugee put in his application.

Now we're in this little two-bedroom heated apartment, we have our own bathroom and kitchen and there's lots of hot water.

After Abugee and I carried the trunk upstairs today and we closed the door behind us, there was a moment where we all looked at each other. Abugee looked at Amigee, Farkhanda looked at me, and then we all laughed.

Amigee took off her coat, pulled off her gloves and said she'd go make us all a cup of tea.

November 23rd, 1964

So much for writing every day. There just isn't time!

I can't believe the principal here wanted to put me in with younger kids! Even with my British marks, somehow they thought I was stupid or something. Abugee finally convinced them not to, and after I aced the test they gave me they finally agreed.

I'm in Grade Eight, and it's going to be tough. The way the boys looked me over when the teacher announced my name was scary.

But I keep my head down and I don't raise my hand, even when I know the answer. They're kind of starting to ignore me, at least in class.

Farkhanda had a hard time of it.

Some boys in her elementary school got hold of her at recess and wouldn't let her go till she threw a rock at a small house. She didn't realize there was a dog sleeping in there. She got bitten three times on her legs and the doctor gave her a needle. Amigee had to go to school to get her, poor little thing.

The next day I told her to show me the ones who did it, and I pinned them down, one by one, and washed their faces with dirt. They'll never do that again!

Now if only I had someone older to beat up my bullies for me.

In terms of teasing, it's just the usual. They call me Zed, or sometimes, when they're being slightly more clever, A-B-C. It was the same in Britain. You'd think that they'd come up with something original!

The trick is not to care. You can't just *pretend* you don't care, you really have to not care. And I don't.

It helps that I learned to fight in England.

Still, I hide my bruises the best I can from Amigee. She's got enough to worry about.

I overheard them talking, late at night when they thought we were asleep. Abugee's having a pretty rough go of it too. They call him "black bastard" at work, and he just takes it!

I'd like to wash *their* faces with dirt!

November 30th, 1964

I finally made a friend! His name is Joe.

He's got dark hair like me, and before I came along they used to pick on him because he's Italian.

I help him with school, and today he took me by his family's restaurant. We never go to restaurants. Amigee doesn't understand why people would. They can make the same food at home much cheaper.

It's the only Italian restaurant on King St. The aromas were like nothing I've ever smelled before.

They had this flat *naan* kind of thing that they'd put some kind of sauce on, and on top of it some other white stuff that turned out to be made from curdled milk like *russ malai*. I asked Joe if there was any pork in it and he said no, this was called cheese. (Cheese comes from milk. It can be really stinky but this one wasn't so bad.)

It was called pizza, with two *z*s but the *z*s aren't pronounced like *zed*. It's more like *peetsa*.

And they had this other stuff that looked like long worms all swirled up in a plate.

I think they should leave that off the menu! I just can't imagine people eating something that looks like worms. He bugged me to taste it, but I just couldn't.

His mother came out of the kitchen, wiping her hands on her apron, and spoke to Joe — in Italian I guess. He answered her, glancing at me from the corner of his eyes. The funniest thing was that his mom kept calling him something else, not Joe, but Giuseppe. He looked embarrassed. When I asked, he told me it meant Joseph. Then I told him that Joseph in our language is Yusuf. He was surprised we had the name too.

Apparently when Joe's family first got here, they had it pretty bad too — that's why he changed his name. What was really weird was that the restaurant was packed with white people all sitting there with their napkins on their laps and knives and forks, cutting up their peetsas and practically drooling over how yummy they were — the same kind of people who'd made Joe's life so hard when he first got here.

It didn't make sense.

I brought him over to our house and he tried some of our *koftas*. He took one bite and started gasping. I thought he was choking till he motioned for the tap. I got him a glass of water, and then another. These people are really sensitive to spices!

I think it's neat that Joe's family decided to open up a restaurant. I like the way they don't hide who they are, at least in the restaurant.

I like the way they're loud and they wave their hands while they talk and they're . . . comfortable.

I wish we were comfortable.

Even at home, we try too hard not to stand out.

We speak in English, even Amigee. The teachers told us to. At first Amigee argued, saying we'd lose our language. Abugee said, "We're here for good. In three generations we'll lose it anyway. It's more important to keep our beliefs."

I told them that Joe's family kept their language. Amigee looked about to argue again, but Abugee just lifted his hand and said, "End of discussion."

And if we talk too loud or Farkhanda runs up and down the hallway, Abugee yells at us. He says the neighbours will think we're a bunch of animals.

One day Amigee burned the spices and Abugee said, "Hurry! Open the windows! The neighbours will smell it!" So we had to put on our coats while the smell cleared out of every open window of the apartment. It took a long time for the apartment to get warm again.

And every day I wait till I come home to pray Zuhr. Abugee told me to. He said not to bother these white people in any way, just go ahead and pray it late. He says God will understand.

But really, what kind of bother would it be to them if I just went in a corner of an empty classroom somewhere and prayed? I could do it during recess. It would take five minutes. It wouldn't hurt anyone.

The Christian missionaries kept their beliefs in Pakistan. When they needed to do something, they just did it.

Why can't we even ask?

Sometimes I think Abugee's too careful.

December 1st, 1964

Everybody's talking about the big scuffle over the flag. I keep my mouth shut at school, but I hope they do change it!

The prime minister wants to put the maple leaf on the flag. That makes a lot more sense than the way it is now! We're not British! Why should we have the Union Jack, even in the corner? We came here to get away from all that!

But a maple leaf, yes! That's Canadian!

December 5ᵗʰ, 1964

Maybe if I'd had a better day I wouldn't have done what I did.

But today was particularly brutal and I just wasn't in the mood for nonsense.

Farkhanda came home singing "Rudolph the Red-nosed Reindeer," for Pete's sake! And from the way she was looking out the window at all the Christmas lights on the houses below, my suspicions were confirmed.

At the dinner table she was still humming it so I said, "Farkhanda believes in Santa Claus!"

Abugee said, "*Behta*, is that true?"

Farkhanda didn't answer. She just stopped chewing her *roti* and swallowed.

Abugee said, "*Behta*, there's no such thing."

I was less gentle. "C'mon, how can a fat man and some reindeer fly?"

Farkhanda mumbled, "They make airplanes fly."

I said, "Then what about all the poor kids? How come they don't just wish for money so they won't be poor anymore?"

Amigee tore a piece of *roti* and dipped it into her

plate of *salan*. She told Farkhanda that this was just a story that parents here tell their children to make them behave. That if they don't be good, then Santa will only bring them a lump of coal.

Farkhanda looked stubborn but didn't say anything.

So I asked her how Santa got into houses that don't have chimneys.

Abugee got a naughty look on his face. He said, "He comes up the toilet."

We all laughed, but Farkhanda didn't. She ran to our room and burst into tears.

I kind of felt sorry for her after a while, and went to calm her down. I told her that it was okay. That if I was younger I'd believe in him too.

She didn't want to be comforted. She just said, "He is too real! And I have proof!"

When I asked her what it was she got stubborn and wouldn't tell me.

December 7ᵗʰ, 1964

I can't believe I made it home in one piece!

Joe was busy so I had to walk home alone. As I passed by the corner store there were four big guys hanging around smoking. They called me that bad name that means negro and told me to go back where I came from.

I glanced at them. Big mistake.

Maybe they saw how scared I was because they chased me.

I couldn't run home — I couldn't show them where

I lived. So I ran down back streets and alleyways and finally lost them, and myself.

It took me two hours to get home.

Amigee was worried sick. She bugged me for ages with questions, but I made up a story and she finally believed it. Didn't want her to worry.

I'll have to find a different route to school.

December 10ᵗʰ, 1964

What does it mean when your little sister draws a picture of herself with white skin?

When I told her she wasn't white, she went crazy.

Amigee told me to leave her alone, but I wasn't in the mood. I said, "Don't be stupid, Abugee's brown and Amigee's brown. Brown parents make brown kids."

Farkhanda said, *"You're* all brown, but I'm *white!"*

So I grabbed her arm and held it against mine. "Look, dummy! They're the same colour!"

She still didn't get it, so I held her up before the bathroom mirror, her face next to mine. "See? We're the same."

The look on her face gave me no pleasure.

December 12ᵗʰ, 1964

Farkhanda took five baths today. One in the morning, one at lunch and three after school.

After every bath she asked me to hold her up to the bathroom mirror.

The fifth time she wanted me to do it, I said I

wouldn't till she told me why she was taking so many baths.

Today they'd read a book called *Harry the Dirty Dog*. Afterwards the other kids told her she was brown because she was dirty.

She was trying to wash the dirt off.

December 15th, 1964

I don't get it. In Pakistan, the kids who had the most honour were the ones with the highest marks.

It's not that I want the other kids to admire me. But it is surprising the way they rush to see what I got, glance at the 97 or 98 at the top of the page, and then turn away like it doesn't matter at all.

And I can't believe how stupid some of them are.

Today was freezing cold. At recess, everyone was huddled into the corners to get out of the wind.

I was too. Didn't they see me? And yet Richard said to the others, "Oh, this cold doesn't bother Zayd."

They all looked at me. I could think of nothing to say.

I was glad when Richard's friend said, "Why?"

I wanted to know too.

Richard said that I came from a hot country and had all that heat bottled up inside me to keep me warm.

They all looked at me again. So I stood a bit straighter, unhunched my shoulders and pretended like it was true.

They actually believed it.

Later on, even Joe nudged me and asked, "Is it true? Do you have the heat all bottled up inside so you don't feel cold?"

I gave him a look.

He said, "How are we supposed to know? You're the first brown guy we've met."

And then we both laughed.

December 16ᵗʰ, 1964

Ha! They changed it! Our new flag has a big fat maple leaf in the middle and red stripes on the side!

Way better than the old one!

December 21ˢᵗ, 1964

Farkhanda's still taking five baths a day.

She thought she was getting lighter at last, but it turned out to be dry skin.

She stopped drinking chocolate milk and doesn't toast her bread either. She figures if she eats white things she'll get white.

We had to go to the Christmas assembly.

Farkhanda was in the Christmas pageant. It was the story of the birth of Jesus (peace be upon him).

They made her pretend to be a Christmas tree.

I can't believe my parents weren't furious.

December 22ⁿᵈ, 1964

Christmas holidays!

No school. No homework. No running from bullies.

Farkhanda's gone back to humming "Rudolph the Red-nosed Reindeer." She spends most of her days looking out the window admiring the Christmas lights.

December 25ᵗʰ, 1964

They must be happy. They got a white Christmas.

It looks like everything is sprinkled with icing sugar.

The streets are deserted.

Farkhanda woke up early. All day she frantically rooted around the house, under the bed, under the sofas, in the kitchen cupboards, behind the coats and boots in the front closet.

She must have searched every inch of the apartment, then she came and plopped down on the sofa.

She stared straight ahead. Nothing on her face moved, except her bottom lip. It was quivering.

As soon as I said, "What's wrong?" she burst into tears.

I told her to shush, but she just cried louder. When I told her Abugee would hear, she shut up a bit.

Finally she told me what was bothering her. "You were right. He isn't real."

She meant Santa Claus.

I thought, "Well, yeah!" but I didn't say so. Then she went to our room, stuck her hand under her pillow and showed me her "proof." In school they'd had to write letters to Santa.

She'd told the teacher she didn't believe in him — he wasn't real. The teacher told her to write a letter anyway. So she'd asked for all the toys she'd ever wanted. A week later the teacher handed out replies — letters from Santa — and Farkhanda was shocked to get one too.

She fingered this rumpled piece of paper. "All the teachers say my name wrong so the other kids laugh. They never say 'Far-*khan*-da' and they spell it in all kinds of ways. See here?" She pointed at the top of the letter. "It's spelled right!"

She crumpled up the letter and threw it away from her.

Then she looked out the window at all the colourful lights on the houses.

She did not sing "Rudolph the Red-nosed Reindeer."

She did not even hum it.

January 1st, 1965

I should be happy. Isn't it a new year with new hopes and new possibilities?

Many of the people are nice, but you just never know when someone will say something. Yesterday I was helping Amigee with the groceries and this gang of kids started following us home.

I hate how scared Amigee looked. She picked up Farkhanda even though she can walk perfectly fine on her own, and rushed along, her eyes rolling back to glance at them.

I was pulling our little grocery cart. If there were only two of those boys and if I were alone, I'd have beat them up for the things they were saying.

Always they tell us to go back where we came from. Sometimes I wish we would.

Sometimes it feels like no matter how hard we try, we'll never belong here. We're not like Joe's family. We're not white enough to blend in.

Every day at school we sing "O Canada, our home and native land . . . " but it doesn't feel like home, and will it ever be our "native" land?

And yet, in a few years, Abugee says we can be citizens. He says we'll have the same rights as everyone else: the right to vote and even the right to complain. That's why we moved here.

But will becoming citizens change the way people feel about us?

January 7ᵗʰ, 1965

Oh my gosh, so much has changed! It happened so suddenly, like it was straight out of a movie.

Joe and I were coming out of the corner store. This lady had just let go of her baby carriage to tie her shoelace, when the dog, this Great Dane or something, whose leash was tied to the carriage, saw a cat and took off after it down the street, dragging the baby carriage behind.

The lady screamed, and started running, but there was no way she could catch the carriage.

The dog was headed for King Street! You could see the cars rushing by!

Joe and I chased it down. It took us ages to catch up. Joe grabbed the dog's leash. I grabbed the carriage handle.

Another few seconds and they would have gone out into traffic or the carriage could have tipped over.

The lady came running up to us, out of breath. She reached in and pulled out the baby, who was screaming his head off.

She called us heroes!

A crowd gathered and she kept telling everyone what we'd done. It was embarrassing, but in a good way.

The lady offered us a reward, but Joe and I just looked at each other. It felt wrong to take it, so we said no, it was okay.

Then someone called the newspaper, and they came and interviewed us both at our homes.

Amigee hugged me real hard, Abugee's eyes were shining and he messed up my hair.

We got our pictures in the paper! They misspelled *Hassan*, writing *Hanson* instead, but still!

January 8th, 1965

Our story was all over the school. In the hallway, some kids I didn't even know came up to say, "Good job!"

In gym I got picked third for a team, even though I'm not very good.

Joe gets a real kick out of retelling the story. Each time he tells it he adds a bit more detail, like how the dog's drool was spraying him, and how the dog snapped at him when he tried to grab the leash and how my hand slipped on the carriage handle (it didn't) and how I almost fell before I caught hold of it. And each time he tells it, where we stopped the carriage gets closer and closer to King Street, till we were inches away. It was more like ten yards.

January 18th, 1965

I feel almost comfortable at school. It's amazing the way some of the kids (especially the girls) look at me now, with shy smiles from the corner of their eyes. The others still want to beat the tar out of me. I'm not surprised a newspaper article didn't change their minds!

And yet what exactly has changed?

I'm still the same person I was before it happened. And what if it hadn't happened? What if I went my whole life without a chance to prove that I was the kind of kid who'd help a lady with her baby carriage?

Would they have eventually come to see that I'm okay?

I guess I'll never know.

But it has changed the way I carry myself at school. And I think that's the main reason I ended up telling Joe about my prayer situation.

He seemed surprised that I'd even care.

I didn't tell him that Dadiami had warned me not to let go of my beliefs. I could see that happening. (It was already happening at the missionary school!)

I just told him that it bugs me to pray late.

He said I should ask Miss Henry.

So I got up the nerve today.

She looked at me funny. "Pray?" she asked, like she hadn't heard me the first time.

"Yeah. I have to pray at certain times, and when I get home it's a bit too late."

She fiddled with some papers on her desk and said, "Well I suppose so. We've never had a request like this before, but I don't see why not."

I can't believe I've been fretting over it all this time, when that's all it took.

Even if she thought I was a bit weird, so what?

I'm glad I asked.

Any other Canadian would have.

*From 1867 to 1967, a hundred thousand Home Children
— so named because they came from Doctor Thomas
Barnardo's homes for orphans and destitute children
in Britain — came to Canada. Some of these "waifs
and strays" found loving homes; others did not.
It is estimated that one-tenth of Canada's population today
is descended from a Home Child.*

IRENE N. WATTS *has written about other Home Children
in her novel* Flower. *Her award-winning play* Lillie
is based on that book.

The Flower of the Flock

ꞩ

The Diary of Harriet James

England to Peterborough, Ontario
June – July 1912

Friday, June 14, 1912
Aboard the Tunisian

It is my first night aboard the ship that is taking orphans to Canada — a perfect time to begin my diary. It was very kind of our house mother at Dr. Barnardo's Girls' Home in Essex to give one to each girl leaving England.

"Write down your thoughts and experiences," she said. "Memories are important." So, here I am, Harriet James, twelve years old, starting out on my big adventure. I'm perched on a top bunk, down in the steerage dormitory. Alice groans in the bunk below mine, ministered to by her small sister, Jane. Many of the girls are plagued by seasickness, but so far I have been spared!

We had a fine send-off. A band played as we climbed onto "The Barnardo Special," the train taking us to Liverpool. A crowd waved and cheered as we boarded the S.S. *Tunisian*. Anyone would think we were royalty instead of uniformed orphan boys and girls! It seems no time at all since the "Canada Lady" gave her talk. Canada sounds like something out of a story book. Fresh air, plentiful food and a beautiful land of rivers, lakes and snow-capped mountains. And best of all — families, waiting to welcome us.

"Who wants to go?" she asked, and one by one we put up our hands, eager for a new and better life. "You are The Flower of the Flock, a credit to our founder, Doctor Barnardo," she said.

I remembered reading the sign he'd put up over the orphanage: NO CHILD EVER REFUSED ADMIS-SION. It's true — none of us are turned away.

I'm too tired to write any more.

Saturday, June 15, 1912

The six o'clock bell woke us and we hurried to dress and line up to wash before prayers and breakfast. This was an unaccustomed feast of tea, porridge, fresh bread and butter, sausages and apples. We were served by stewards in white jackets! Our supervisor read out the rules:

Do not to speak to the Crew members, keeping them
from their work.
No running or shouting in the corridor or on deck.
Do not climb the railings on deck.

We are accustomed to rules and regulations, and punishment if we disobey. But for the next eight days we will have no chores, and may walk and play on deck.

This morning I woke up shivering with excitement — as if I was about to discover an orange in my stocking on Christmas morning! Was Thomas on this ship too? Was this the day that I'd find him? If Thomas is on board, we'll find each other. After all, we think the same thoughts and sometimes even dream the same dreams, the way twins do. I found out that we're the third shipment of Home Children out this year, so Angus might not be far behind Thomas.

Later

Thomas is here! It's hard to believe, but it's true. I'll try to set down just how it happened.

After lunch, instead of joining a skipping game on deck, I sat with my back against one of the iron ladders and waited. (Please, *please* let Thomas be here.) My lips tasted salty. I breathed in the tang of the sea air and watched the creamy white crests of the waves.

My thoughts drifted like the clouds overhead . . . To the two years since I have seen my brothers and since Mother died. The two years since Father brought Thomas, Angus and me to the London orphanage at Stepney Causeway. How Angus cried and cried, burying his head against me. "It looks like a *prison*, Harry," he sobbed. It did, with its high grey walls. And then they parted us. Two years is far too long — I need Thomas. I need them both.

Father had told us that we'd be taken care of, that it was better than the workhouse. He said he was going up north to find work, and promised he'd come to get us when he got back on his feet again. But he never did.

My thoughts turned to that awful day three months ago when I was called into the office and told Father had died in an accident. That day, of all days, I wanted to be with my brothers in London, not apart from them at the Girls' Home. That was the moment we truly became orphans. Before, it hadn't been true. We were not like some of the other Barnardo children.

But just then someone tugged at my braid and I whipped around.

"Harriet James! *Harry!* I've been looking all over for you."

"Tom, it's *you!*" I jumped up and hugged him. It was like looking into my own face to see him — his red hair, freckles and green eyes like an alley cat's, just like mine. We huddled down, sheltered from the breeze and from prying eyes.

"You've grown," I said, noticing how he was taller than I am now. Then I asked where Angus was.

Thomas never lies, even though he knows how hard this is for me to hear. He told me Angus didn't get on the Canada list this time, because he is still too small for an eight year old and he coughed all winter. When I looked worried, Thomas told me not to fret, because Angus is Matron's pet. And he'll have his chance when he's stronger. "He'll be fine," Tom added..

He must have seen my eyes well up, for he whispered that he'd meet me here tomorrow, same time. "You know they don't like boys talking to girls — not even to their sisters," he said. "And I'm late for a talk about

Canadian wildlife." With that he sprinted away.

I comforted myself that if we'd all stayed in England, Tom would soon be apprenticed, and I'd be going into service. We'd still be apart — though not with a whole ocean between us.

Friday, June 21, 1912

I have been neglecting my diary. In the evenings, settled in our bunks, we girls whisper our hopes and dreams of the family that will take us in. The ship rocks me to sleep before I have even picked up my pencil.

This morning one of the sailors shouted that whales had been sighted to starboard. Everyone screamed and ran to look for a sight of the huge creatures, blowing spray and keeping pace with the ship. Two of the boys climbed astride the railings to get a closer look. A sailor grabbed them, a whistle blew and they were sent below in disgrace. We later found out the reason for the "no climbing on railings" rule — a Barnardo boy had drowned on one of the earlier crossings, washed over the rails by a giant wave.

Saturday, June 22, 1912

We arrive in Quebec, Canada, tomorrow. Thomas and I found a few minutes to talk late yesterday, in that same sheltered spot where we couldn't be easily seen. He told me the boys will go to a Barnardo's Home in Toronto, before being sent on to families as far away as

Winnipeg or Vancouver. I saw a map pinned up on the ship. How can a country be so big? It looks as vast as an ocean. The girls go to Peterborough. Who knows when Thomas and I will meet again? Only one week together, after two years apart — and how will I know where he is?

Have we done right to come so far from home, Tom? I wondered.

"Father would say that we're going to a better life, Harry," he said.

We laughed then because he'd read my thoughts, the way he sometimes can — answering my question before I've even spoken!

Thomas promised to find me once we reached our destinations. And we agreed we had to do the best with the chance we've been given to make a better life.

We walked round the deck once more. The supervisors soften their hearts today and take no notice of us, letting us have some last moments together.

The lump in my throat won't go away.

Tuesday, June 25, 1912
Canada

Yesterday, we landed in Canada! The wait to be passed by the doctor in the immigration shed was agony. The girl ahead of me in the line was held back. Her eyes are infected, so she'll be sent back to England. "Trachoma," the doctor murmured to the nurse.

I was trembling so much when it was my turn that he

smiled. "I am not in the habit of eating little girls," he said. The nurse beside him laughed and I was waved through! Hours later, we were marched to the railway station and onto the train to continue our journey.

When we reached Toronto, the boys got off. I saw Thomas turn around to wave goodbye . . . The thought of another separation is hard to bear. But we'd said we'd make the best of things. I'm willing myself not to cry as I write this.

Later

The wheels go round. . . . They echo my thoughts — *far from home, far from home.* I watch the scenery go by. The skies are as blue and endless as the ocean. Animals graze peacefully. Houses are scattered far apart. I am the only one still awake. Alice and Jane sleep, holding hands, afraid of being separated.

Wednesday, June 26, 1912
Peterborough, Ontario

As soon as the guard announced "Peterborough," we gathered our things and tumbled out onto the platform. People stared as though we were strange animals. A short drive brought us to Hazelbrae, the Barnardo Girls' Home. It is a fine-looking white mansion, ringed by beautiful trees. We were shown to an annex added onto the back of the house. This is where we will eat and sleep. Matron welcomed us and said a short prayer before we ate our supper of soup, bread and cocoa.

Settled at last on my narrow cot, all of us crowded close together in the long dormitory, I am still dazed from travelling. My pillow is soft and white — time to close my diary.

Thursday, June 27, 1912
Hunter Street, Peterborough

This morning after a breakfast of oatmeal — as porridge is called in Canada — bread and tea we were assigned chores. Mine was to sweep the dormitories. Every few minutes, girls came up to fetch their bags, then hurried down to waiting strangers who had come to pick them up. I felt nervous, waiting for my turn. Would my new family like me?

At lunch I managed to sit next to Alice. I guessed how badly she must feel. Her sister had been collected earlier today. Jane had sobbed, "Tell Alice I love her," when she came up to the dormitory to collect her things. I was nearly in tears myself. I knew how much they wanted to stay together. All I could do was put my arms round Jane and wish her luck in her new home.

Alice told me she had been dusting the main entrance hall when Jane was fetched. She ran out to wave goodbye, desperate to know where her little sister was going. We all know that's the rule — no one ever gets told. Alice whispered in my ear that she did not think that was right!

Later

Before Alice could tell me more, I was called into the office and introduced to a Miss Hawthorn, who had come for me. As we travelled to my new home, I discovered that she is a dressmaker who lives with her widowed mother. Also, that her younger brother had been married last winter.

The buggy stopped in front of a fine yellow brick house with a gabled roof. The driver carried my trunk round the back of the house. Roses bloom in the front garden and two fine elm trees stand on either side of the house. Miss Hawthorn said her father had planted those trees when he was a boy. We went indoors, and she opened the door to her sewing room.

Miss Hawthorn speaks and moves fast, as though she is afraid of being interrupted! "It will be your responsibility to keep my workroom impeccable, and to pick up any stray pins. The sewing machine is always covered when not in use!" she told me. Next, I was taken into the parlour to meet Mrs. Hawthorn. She holds herself like a queen. Her hair is snowy white, her eyes a piercing blue. Her hand gripped a slim black cane and a fine ring glittered on her finger.

"There you are at last, Tabitha," she said. "I was just about to ring for Mrs. Baines. So this is the Home Girl."

She asked me to show her my hands. I did so and she told me to pour her some water from the covered pitcher on the table. I handed Mrs. Hawthorn her glass, careful not to spill a single drop. I bobbed a curtsy. "My name is Harriet James, ma'am," I said.

She ignored me and turned to her daughter. "I have asked Mrs. Baines to serve tea on the back porch in half an hour."

Miss Hawthorn took me up to an attic at the top of the house. My trunk was there and I was told to unpack and then go down to the kitchen to help Mrs. Baines, the cook/housekeeper.

A room of my own! A sloping roof, a narrow bed covered with a patchwork quilt, and a window from which I can see the back garden. There is a chest, hooks on the wall and a chair beside my bed. I unpacked quickly, and put on a clean apron.

Mrs. Baines, her hands covered in flour, looked up from her mixing bowl and said I could help myself to a glass of milk from a jug in the larder. "Do as you're told, and you and I will get on fine," she said. "They tell me you orphan girls are good workers. I don't live in. Monday to Saturday, I arrive in the morning, cook breakfast and stay until supper is prepared. Miss Hawthorn comes down about seven each morning, and likes the tea made. Three spoons in the pot, girl, so she can bring a cup to her mother while I serve their breakfasts."

Everyone in Canada talks so fast. I hope I can remember all my duties.

"I'm used to getting up at six, Mrs. Baines, and to making tea," I said.

She answered that I was not like Ruby, then, who was hard to get up on winter mornings. That she'd left last week after two years' service to join her sister in Toronto. It seems Mrs. Hawthorn was not pleased. When I asked Mrs. Baines if Ruby was an orphan too, she replied that I was the first girl who'd been hired from an orphanage. I was told to prepare vegetables for supper, and to set the table for the ladies.

After I had finished serving them, I ate my supper at the kitchen table. Mrs. Baines had left me a plate, generously heaped with food. I cleaned the kitchen and mopped the floor. Then I made sure that the sewing room was neat before I went to bed. I heard Mrs. Hawthorn's stick tapping from room to room. She was checking that everything was in order.

I'm grateful for my food. I like work. But it's not the family I was promised.

Have you found a good place, Tom, and a room of your own like mine? If only I knew where you are! You could be thousands of miles away. I can't bear to think of it. How will you keep your promise to find me, then? I hope someone has spoken a word of welcome to you.

I'll close the diary before my tears smudge these pages again.

Sunday, June 30, 1912

Mr. and Mrs. Charles Hawthorn — he is Mrs. Hawthorn's son — and their little girl, Lizzie, came for tea after church. Mrs. Baines and I had baked strawberry tartlets and scones in readiness and she told me that Lizzie was actually Mr. Charles's stepdaughter. Her mother had been widowed when Lizzie was a year old.

No sooner had I brought in the tea when the little girl knocked over her lemonade. Mrs. Hawthorn looked cross. The child's lips trembled. I hurried out and returned with clean cloths and the table was soon put to rights.

Miss Tabitha told me to take Lizzie out into the garden. I said Lizzie might call me Harry, as my brothers did. We went outside and played hide-and-seek — I've always liked looking after little ones — until her mother came to say it was time to go home. Lizzie wanted to stay and play with me. Her mother smiled and thanked me nicely for looking after her. It made feel a little less lonely to receive a kind word. How I would have loved to go home with them! I heard Lizzie's high voice asking her mother why I could not go and play in their house.

Monday, July 1, 1912
Dominion Day

Today is a holiday. By early afternoon my chores were done. Mrs. Hawthorn and Miss Tabitha had gone to Victoria Park to hear the band concert and to share a picnic lunch with Mr. Charles and his family.

I made my way to the park too. Families sat on the lawn below the white bandstand, the ladies shaded from the sun by bright parasols and wide-brimmed hats.

"Harry!" a little voice called and I saw Lizzie running towards me. "Why didn't you come to the picnic? We had chicken and cake and oranges!"

I told her she was a lucky girl — that I had never been on a picnic.

Mrs. Charles caught up with her daughter. "Lizzie has taken such a liking to you, Harriet," she said.

I felt myself blush at the compliment. To think she had remembered my name! She took Lizzie to look at the fountain, and wished me a pleasant day.

I curtsied, turned away, and almost immediately saw Alice coming towards me. I had not expected to see her again. She said that Matron has kept her on at Hazelbrae to wait on the staff. Alice hopes to find out where Jane is, in spite of the rules. She walked back to Hunter Street with me. I begged her to try to find out where Thomas has been sent.

Almost dawn

A summer storm woke me in the middle of the night. Wind rattled the window. I jumped out of bed, closed the window and watched lightning zigzag across the sky before I huddled down in my bed again.

Tuesday, July 2, 1912

Mrs. Hawthorn stayed in bed with a migraine — the thunder had kept her awake. Her bell rang constantly, and I carried trays up to her and then back down.

Miss Tabitha sent me to tidy her storeroom next to my attic. The room buzzed with heat and bluebottles. I sorted boxes of remnants, patterns and Eaton's catalogues. The catalogues are so beautiful. They advertise the latest fashions, household goods and toys. A red fire engine in a Christmas catalogue made me long for Angus.

After I'd finished, Miss Tabitha sent me to exchange her mother's library book. It felt good to be outside. The boardwalks had dried off after the rain.

This was the first time I've ever been inside a library. The man behind the counter, who introduced himself as Mr. Delafosse, the librarian, read Miss Tabitha's note. He said that *The Prisoner of Zenda* is an exciting adventure story, then asked me if I was visiting and did I enjoy reading too. When I said I was an orphan from England, he said he had the perfect book for me. It is called *Anne of Green Gables* by L.M. Montgomery. The girl on the cover has red hair like me!

I was given a library card. I was told I must return it signed by an adult, but meanwhile the librarian let me borrow the book! And there is nothing to pay. Imagine, books for anyone to read! This has turned out to be a wonderful day.

Later

Tonight I found out that Anne is an orphan too. I wonder if it is worse to have brothers I might never see again, or never to have had any at all.

Saturday, July 6, 1912

I think I may have seen Thomas today!

It is market day and Mrs. Baines sent me to buy

lemons. She warned me not to waste time — guests were expected and the lemonade had to be ready. After I bought the lemons, I swear I glimpsed Thomas on the far side of the Market Hall. But just then the lady beside me jostled my arm and I dropped the change. The coin had rolled behind the stall and by the time I found it, the red-haired boy was out of sight. I ran up and down looking for him, calling Thomas's name, but the market was full of shoppers and I was afraid to be late getting back. Even though I rushed home, Mrs. Baines scolded me for taking so long, and found me chore after chore to do.

I comforted myself that it probably hadn't been Thomas after all. What would he be doing in Peterborough?

Wednesday, July 10, 1912

Miss Tabitha is extra busy making dresses for two summer weddings. They have to be complete by August. So it is late before I can tidy the room.

Mrs. Hawthorn came into the sewing room as I was picking up stray pins, startling me. "I have rung for you twice. Too *busy* reading the catalogues, I see," she said. I explained that I had just been putting them in order. She asked where her daughter was and I replied that she had gone for a stroll, because the evening was so pleasant.

"I did not ask you for a weather report, girl. Bring some tea to the parlour when you have finished," she snapped.

I don't know what I have done to displease her. She watches my every move, waiting for me to do something wrong.

Thursday, July 11, 1912

Mrs. Baines said that tomorrow the ladies will accompany Mr. Charles and his wife to the Grand Opera. They will dine out first. This means I'll have the evening to read! I can't wait to find out what happens after Anne dyes her hair!

Mrs. Baines thinks that "an important announcement" will soon be made. When I looked confused, she confided that Mrs. Charles is expecting. Will a new grandchild make Mrs. Hawthorn any kinder?

Friday, July 12, 1912

While the ladies were at breakfast, I finished cleaning the bedrooms and had got started on the downstairs windows when I was sent upstairs again to Mrs. Hawthorn.

"Come here," she ordered.

What had I done this time? I'd pressed her white wrap to perfection, even Mrs. Baines said so. Had a speck of dust been discovered?

"I warned my daughter not to take in a girl from the streets!" she said, brandishing her stick. "My pearl necklace is missing. You are the *only* person who could have taken it."

I am not like Anne Shirley and I won't make up a false

confession. "I am not a thief, ma'am," I managed to say. But her pinched mouth told me she didn't believe me at all.

"Tell me where it is, and if you have not come to your senses by tomorrow afternoon, I shall have to summon the Constable," she said.

She terrified me. Her eyes bored into my face, she thumped her cane on the floor, and I feared she was going to strike me. Then she told me to leave her presence. The rest of the day was the worst I can remember. Everyone shunned me — even Mrs. Baines would not meet my eyes. What was my word against that wicked woman upstairs?

That night after everyone had left for the opera, I made a decision. How can I stay in a home where I am branded as a thief, without any proof? What good is food and a room, when I am not even called by my name? *"Do this, girl."* That's all I am to them — the girl from the streets. I hoped Matron would understand. I packed my trunk and planned to tell Miss Tabitha next day that I wished to return to Hazelbrae.

Lunch was over. I had dried and put away the dishes — almost dropping a platter, my hands shook so much, in anticipation of another interview with Mrs. Hawthorn. My apron was still damp when Mrs. Baines sent me upstairs to the old lady. But I deliberately refused to change my apron — Mrs. Hawthorn had called me a thief, turned everyone against me, and did not deserve my respect.

I knocked on the door, and stood before her. She asked me if I had anything to say. I shook my head. At that moment I knew I could not utter a sound.

"Well? So you have come to your senses then? Better the truth than a prison sentence, is that it?"

My words flowed then; I had no trouble at all in voicing them. "I'm a poor girl, yes, ma'am, but in my whole life I have never taken anything that did not belong to me, not so much as a piece of bread! I swear that I did not take your necklace."

Mrs. Hawthorn raised her stick at me and stood up so hastily that the cushion she'd been leaning against slipped down. She turned to move it and I saw the pearl necklace, gleaming on the chair. Mrs. Hawthorn was speechless for a full minute. Then she mumbled that the clasp must have come undone when she'd tried on the necklace. She dismissed me and told me to get on with my work. Instead, I ran up to my room and cried and cried, longing for Thomas to rescue me. You *promised*, I sobbed.

Saturday, July 13, 1912

Dear Diary, I never thought I would be writing words like this. Nothing is as it was yesterday — everything has changed.

Mrs. Hawthorn caught the afternoon train to Lindsay yesterday. She had planned to visit with friends for a while. I hope I never have to see her again. Her and her suspicious eyes and her false accusations. I was ready to speak to Miss Tabitha about deciding to leave, but before I had a chance to do that, she sent for me.

I can hardly believe this myself, but Miss Tabitha did not mention her mother or the necklace at all. Instead she said that Mrs. Charles had asked if Mrs. Hawthorn could spare me to work as a mother's help for Lizzie and the new baby! She thought I had a way with children! She said that Lizzie had never taken to anyone outside the family before. It would do her good to have an older girl to look up to. Also, it would free Mrs. Charles to concentrate on the new baby.

I waited, holding my breath.

She went on to say that, fortunately, Mrs. Baines has a niece seeking employment, so no one will be inconvenienced by my leaving. Mr. Charles would collect me after church tomorrow.

I thanked her and returned to the kitchen, not daring to believe in my good fortune!

Later

Mrs. Baines and I were having a cup of tea, when suddenly there was a knock on the door. Mrs. Baines opened it.

A voice said, "Please, ma'am, I've come to see my sister."

I knew that voice — Thomas! I threw my arms around his neck.

"Harry, stop choking me," he laughed.

Mrs. Baines collapsed onto a chair, fanning herself with a tea cloth.

"Twins! As alike as two peas in a pod!" she exclaimed.

Tom explained that he had to get back to the market stall — he'd been given only an hour or so to look for me. I asked Mrs. Baines if I could walk a little way with my brother. She put a basket in my hand and gave me a quarter, saying she needed eggs, though I knew there were six in the larder! I felt like hugging her too. *He's kept his promise,* I wanted to sing and shout. *This is my brother!*

On our way to market I told Tom all about the Hawthorns and how happy I was to be going to my new place. He told me he lives on the outskirts of Peterborough — in Ashburnham — not far at all. He told me he loved farming — everything about it: feeding chickens, cleaning out the pigsty, milking, and especially going to market every Saturday to lift crates and sell and deliver produce. Farmer Hughes and his wife treat him more like a son than a hired hand, he said.

"How in the world did you find me, Tom?" I asked him.

He said that it was Alice who answered the door at Hazelbrae when he came by to ask for me. She told him where I lived and he ran all the way here.

By the time he'd explained everything, we were at the market. I was sad to reach the produce stall so soon! There was still so much to tell each other.

"This is my sister Harriet, Mrs. Hughes," Tom said, introducing me.

She shook my hand and smiled warmly and said she was happy we had found each other. And if I happened to be passing by one Saturday, she might see her way to spare Tom for a little while. She ruffled his hair fondly.

Tuesday, July 16, 1912
George Street, Peterborough

Already I feel as if I belong to a real family. Lizzie is my little shadow! Mrs. Charles wants to come to market to meet Thomas.

I will get a dollar a month to spend, and my first purchase will be a one-penny stamp, so that I may write to Angus. I shall tell him that both Tom and I have found good homes. I will write how much we miss him and hope he too may come to Canada one day.

A case of tonsillitis means that Insy has to go for help,
far from her father's trapline. Travelling out of the bush
takes her on a surprising journey to a very
different world.

RUBY SLIPPERJACK grew up in the bush north
of Lake Superior. She still spends as much time
on the land — a place that features strongly in all
her stories — as she can.

The Charleston at the Trapline

∾

The Diary of Insy Pimash

Northwestern Ontario
February 1924

Monday, February 4, 1924

First page in my new journal.

Mama just changed the cedar poultice around my throat and gave me some more medicine tea to keep my fever down. I have tonsillitis. I had to look up the word in an old dictionary Mama has.

My throat is very sore. My head hurts too. Mama just came back into the cabin with an armload of wood, letting in a cloud of cold air when she opened the door. Eli is outside sawing wood with the handsaw. I can hear him whistling — he always whistles when he's doing something. Nina is over by the window with her doll. I can't see what she's doing from here. I'm going to try to sleep now.

Tehteh just got back from checking his traps. The first thing he did when he walked in was to come over to my bed and put his hand on my head.

I've been listening to my parents talking. It's sounding like Tehteh has to take me to the hospital. I can hear Eli and Nina running around outside and laughing — probably playing with the dogs. Mama's frying fish, but I don't feel hungry.

I like the green yarn that Mama used to sew together the cut pages of paper for my new journal.

Tuesday, February 5
Lunch Break

Mama dressed me really warm this morning and Tehteh put a canvas over the sled and several blankets and put a backrest frame at the back so I could lean against it. He wrapped me up in the blankets and tied me to the sled like a big bundle. Boogy and Patch were already tied to the dogsled harness. Those two really like to run. They're always excited to be going somewhere.

It was still dark when we left home. I watched the sun come up when we were crossing the second lake. It was nice and the ride was smooth until we came up to a long portage. The bumpy ride was really hard on my swollen throat. On smooth parts of the trail, Tehteh stood on the back runners of the sled behind me, but he would jump down and run, pushing the sled with a pole, whenever the dogs went uphill. I couldn't see him from where I was sitting, but I know he would be dragging the pole to the right side when he wanted the dogs to turn right, and whistling once to make them turn left.

We stopped for lunch about halfway and rested the dogs. I couldn't eat anything, so Tehteh made me some tea porridge, which I was able to swallow. He also heated my poultice in a frying pan!

At Old Man Mee-shichiimin's Cabin

We finally came into the clearing to the community of Flint Lake and Tehteh stopped at the first cabin we came to. The old man who lives here always takes care of Tehteh's dogs when he comes in for supplies.

I am lying on the old man's bed now, writing this. Tehteh has gone to the General Store to trade in the furs he brought with us, for cash. Tehteh also brought big chunks of moose meat for the old man. The old man is now whistling happily away and cooking some on his wood stove. His name, Mee-shichiimin, is a kind of bristly berry, but I do not know the English name for it. Suits him well, I think.

I must have dozed off again. Tehteh is back from the store and food is steaming on the table. The old man came and gave me a bowl. He had made moose broth and thin dumplings for me. I ate the whole thing. The old man wanted to know why I was scribbling on these papers and Tehteh told him that Mama wanted me to write down everything I see so I don't miss the writing lessons she makes me do each day.

On the Train

Right after the meal, Tehteh switched his moccasins for a pair of boots and carried me piggyback to the train station. I was not feeling well enough to notice much. There were a lot of people in the waiting room though. I lay on one of the benches against the wall. There was a stove in the corner — a tall stand-up kind. The ticket agent worked behind the counter with a pencil tucked above his left ear. I wondered how it stayed put.

I got really scared when the noise of the train got louder, but I didn't see the engine. We went out when the train stopped. Once inside the train, we found two bench seats facing each other and we settled in. The conductor came by when the train started moving and Tehteh gave him our tickets. He was very friendly. He knew right away that I was sick.

Tehteh just gave me some water to drink. I can see a stove at the other end of the coach. It smells of old cigar smoke in here. I am lying on the bench and Tehteh is sitting across from me. There's a constant drone of voices around us. Once in a while, I hear the engine whistle far ahead, but the constant *clickity-clack* and rocking motion is making me sleepy.

I can tell my fever is high again. Tehteh has put a cold wet towel over my forehead. We'd left the poultice at the old man's place and all I had was the towel around my throat.

At the Hospital

It was growing dark when the train stopped at Ojibwe Hill. There was a driver waiting for us when we got off the train and he drove us to the Indian Zone Hospital. The automobile was big and black and box-like. It jolted past the lights on the roads and gave us a very bumpy ride. It was much worse than the dogsled ride through the portages! It really hurt my throat. This was my first time riding in an automobile. I think I prefer riding in the dogsled.

When we got to the hospital, a nurse took me to a large bathroom where there was a nice warm bathtub already filling. She stayed to help me wash my hair with a nice-smelling shampoo. She left a gown and housecoat for me to put on and a pair of booties for my feet. When she returned, she brought a wheelchair for me to sit on because I was feeling dizzy, and she combed my hair. She said her name was Annie. Then she pushed me out and along the hallway until we came to the room where I would stay. There were two beds, one in the corner, but I took the bed by the windows so that I could look outside.

Tehteh is sitting on a chair beside my hospital bed. We're waiting for the doctor. Tehteh looks very tired and his eyes are red, but he smiles at me when he sees me looking at him. He rubs my feet and says *"oshibii-igen"* — telling me to continue writing (but, I am too tired to write any more, so this is what I have written).

The Examination Room

Nurse Annie came in a little while later with the wheelchair, saying that the doctor was ready to see me. Tehteh wheeled me down the hallway, following the nurse. We didn't have to wait long. The doctor was young, with sparkles in his eyes. He listened to my chest with the . . . the thing in his ears — I don't know what that is called. Then, one look at my throat and he knew what was wrong with me. He said that I was not to eat or drink anything because they would be taking my tonsils out first thing in the morning. Then Tehteh wheeled me back to the room.

Later, Nurse Annie came and told Tehteh that she would show him where he could sleep and eat his meals. He came back just before bedtime. He said they have a storage room of some kind in the basement with beds in it. There were four other Ojibwe men there who were waiting for family to get well enough to go home. They eat in an area off the kitchen with two caretakers who live there.

Wednesday, February 6

Tehteh stayed beside my bed until I went to sleep last night. The nurses came to check on me once in a while. Now I can hear plates and glasses rattling down the hallway and I can smell food. It is early morning. I can just see a grey shade through the windows. Tehteh arrived just as an empty cot was rolled into the room to take me to the operating room. I got very scared until he took my hand

and told me *"soongaendun"* — be brave. I wonder when the nurse will come to wheel me off to the operating room.

After the Operation

I opened my eyes and there was Tehteh sitting beside me. I've been sleeping a lot today. He pushed the hair off my forehead and whispered that I did really well and the tonsils were out and the doctor told him that I would be fine. A nurse showed up and they rolled the cot back to my room and got me back into my bed.

When I woke up again, Tehteh was there looking out the window. He gestured to a tray at the foot of the bed. He came and sat down beside me and opened the lid. It was lunchtime and they had given me a bowl of broth and a big mound of jelly and apple juice. My head felt much better. I could tell my fever was gone, but my throat was very sore. I swallowed the broth, but took my time with the jelly. It was red but I could not tell if it was strawberry or raspberry. Tehteh smiled and said, *"minopagon?"* I nodded yes, it was really, really good!

After I wrote that, I fell back to sleep. When I woke up again, Tehteh was sitting in the chair with his back to me, looking out the windows. I could tell from the dim light that it was late afternoon. Then he turned around and faced me. I looked at him and I could feel my face stretch into a smile and he grinned back at me. He had shaved his moustache! He had even had a haircut!

I could hear the rattling plates and glasses coming

down the hallway again. The smell of the food was wonderful, but when Tehteh opened the lid on the tray, it was more jelly, juice and a mound of white stuff. I hesitantly opened my mouth when Tehteh brought the spoon toward me, saying *"miichin"* — insisting that I eat it. He said it is called rice pudding. It was really good! I ate everything. I told Tehteh *"ando wiisinin kaygeen"* and he left, saying that, yes, he would go and eat too. He promised he would be right back.

Later

Nurse Annie came into the room and nodded at my note pages and asked how I learned to write so well. I told her that Mama taught me and that she had learned it from a missionary couple on James Bay. Because Nurse Annie seemed interested, I told her that they had looked after my mama after her Cree parents died when Mama was ten. Then Mama worked as a maid for the old missionary's wife. She was the one who taught Mama English and to learn to read and write. I even told her that the old woman's wedding gift to Mama when she and Tehteh got married was a wooden box full of books that Tehteh had to carry over many portages up the Albany River to the Ojibwe territory, where his trapline was. Once there, Mama taught Tehteh English and he taught her Ojibwe.

Nurse Annie said she really liked that story. Then she asked me why I call my father Tehteh, so I told her that it just means "father." She said goodbye to me then and gave me a hug because she wouldn't be working when it was time for me to go home in the morning. She even gave me a couple of pencils so I wouldn't run out!

Later on, another nurse came and got us and we went back into the examination room. The same young doctor appeared and this time he talked to me instead of Tehteh and he told me that I could go home in the morning.

Just before Tehteh left to go to bed, he told me that he was very busy while I was asleep in the afternoon. He had walked to town and gone into the big store there and bought a small gift for everyone in the family. He had also bought some supplies and packed everything into two boxes that he had left at the train station's baggage area. They would be loaded on the train with us tomorrow morning.

Thursday, February 7
Leaving the Hospital: The Train Station Waiting Room

An older nurse came and flicked the lights on when it was still dark outside! I blinked and then got very excited when I remembered it was time to go home! She put a pile of folded clothes at the bottom of my bed. I asked where my own clothes were, because what she had were city clothes that white people wore. She said the laundry people throw all the clothes that people come in with into the furnace. She said that there was a whole room full of donated clothing that had been washed and ironed and she just placed an order for a twelve-year-old girl's clothes. I told her that I was almost thirteen, but she looked at me and said that I was actually smaller than a regular twelve-year-old girl.

I was not too happy and I did not like her very much. She left saying I only had a few minutes to get dressed. I yanked on the pair of stockings, pulled up a pair of under-pants, a cotton under-dress over my head and then I held up a really nice pink flowered shift dress with lace on the neck and sleeves. I liked it. It was a bit baggy, but it was really pretty! Then I pulled on a pair of boots that laced up the front. They were very uncomfortable. The last thing was a long city coat that wrapped over to one side with a really big shiny button, and then I jammed the matching hat on my head.

I marched out the door and I could see Tehteh stand-ing at the nurse's station at the other end of the hallway. I walked fast toward him and as he turned to look me up and down, I slowed. I heard him say to a young nurse with short hair and cropped bangs, who was leaning over the counter to look at me, "She is going home by dogsled to a trapper's cabin, way up north. Do you think she's going to make it dressed like that?" He smiled at her and she put a hand over her mouth, giggling. While we wait-ed for the driver, the nurses turned up the radio behind the counter and started swinging their arms and legs — a dance they said was called the Charleston. It looked really fun! I memorized every move. I'm going to try that when I get home.

When the driver appeared, the young nurse gave me my medicine. It was a pink fluid in a bottle and she told me to make sure I took one teaspoon three times a day until it was all gone. She handed us two paper lunch bags and we were on our way to that same big, black, box-like automobile, only this time it took us back to the train station. We passed by the restaurant window next door and I saw people sitting at tables eating breakfast. I tugged at Tehteh's coat to see if we could go in, but he just shook his head. It is very loud and busy in the waiting room here.

On the Train

When the train finally came, it hissed and squealed very loudly — like a huge metal monster!! I hung on to Tehteh's hand very hard as the train shook the floor. Many people got on the train, and again we took our seats at the back. Tehteh flipped the backrest to the other side so that his bench now faced mine.

When the train was in motion again, the conductor came by to collect the tickets. I was busy writing when he suddenly leaned over me and asked how I was feeling. I looked up and realized that it was the same man who had been very nice to us. I said that I was doing very well now, and thanked him for asking. He noticed my notepad and he smiled and said that I must be a very smart girl to be able to handwrite so evenly. Then he patted his pockets and came up with a bag of candies from his shirt pocket and handed them to me. I thanked him and as he turned to move away, he paused to ask Tehteh how I had learned to write like that and all

Tehteh said was, "Her mother." People were still moving around, taking off coats and lighting up cigars, and women were chatting by the stove. Tehteh patted my bench and said "*neebaan*" — so I went to sleep.

I woke up and Tehteh was sound asleep in front of me with his coat rolled into a pillow under his head. He really looked different without his moustache. He's always had a moustache.

The train was still rolling along with its endless *clickity-clack*. Then I noticed that it was beginning to slow down. I sat up and looked out the window. The sun was just rising over the trees. I remembered my brown lunch bag and pulled it from under my coat, which was draped over me. I looked inside and there was apple juice, a container of rice pudding and a muffin. I decided to eat that yummy rice pudding first, making sure that I took sips of the juice with it. My throat was tender, but not throbbing with pain anymore. Tehteh woke up when the train stopped. We were in the middle of nowhere. I didn't see any houses at all. I happened to look at the clean slope of white snow over a rock when I saw a rabbit hop out of the bushes and run up the slope and come to a sudden stop right across from my window. I pointed to the rabbit just as Tehteh sat up. It sat there looking at the train. When the train lurched forward again with a lot of clanging and banging, the rabbit whirled and high-tailed it back into the bush. I saw a huge tank thing go by on the other side of the train windows — maybe that is what we had to stop for — whatever that was.

I think I will save the muffin for our lunch stop on the way home. Tehteh says we should be there soon.

Back at Old Man's Cabin

When we got off the train, Tehteh made me stay inside the waiting room until the train pulled out. Then he came in with one box under each arm and we hurried down the railway tracks to the old man's place. As we neared the cabin, Boogy and Patch saw us and they were jumping up at the end of their chains, yipping. Their back ends were shaking from wagging their tails so fast! I ran and hugged them and they licked my face!

Tehteh was already inside when I got to the door. I stepped inside to see that the old man was by the stove and he turned and, with raised bushy eyebrows, he pointed at my clothes. Then he began a rasping hissing laugh that shook his shoulders! On impulse, I twirled around and did a good curtsy for him. Now his rasping took on a louder hiss as he clapped his hands and a gaping hole appeared on his bristly whiskered face. Then Tehteh went *tsk, tsk, tsk, "ta-gibichita-eh"* — so I stopped. Tehteh was right. No reason to give the old man a heart attack.

I went to the bed and took off the coat and silly boots. The old man had a meal of rabbit stew with dumplings ready for us. He told Tehteh that he was saving the moose meat for the long weeks until he would see him again — I guess Tehteh always brings him meat or fish when he comes into the community for supplies. The old man gave me a bowl of rabbit broth and lots of soft dumplings. It was delicious. They talked by the table for a while until Tehteh had to leave to go to the General Store to get some warm clothes for me.

At the Lunch Stop

When Tehteh got back from the store, he was in a hurry to leave so we could make it back to our cabin before dark. He brought back a wool sweater that I pulled on over my dress, and I stuffed my skirt into a pair of boys' thick wool pants with a buttoned hole in front. While Tehteh switched his boots back to his moccasins, I pulled on two pairs of boys' work socks. He couldn't find any boots my size at the store, so he bought a pair of boys' high, thick boot liners and tied them onto my feet with two-yard-long oil-lamp wicks. They were just like thick mukluks. Since I was going to be tied back into the canvas and blanket bag, I was going to be warm enough. The last thing to put on was the thick green parka he had bought. It had a wide hood with a thick fur fringe that would protect my face from the wind while crossing the lakes. Finally, I was ready to go, so Tehteh wrapped me up again and tied me to the sled.

The dogs were just bursting to go. With one last wave to the old man, Tehteh jumped on the back of the sled runners behind me and we were off. The dogs were running flat out when we hit the first lake, and soon we were up into another portage. Even with the lunch stop, we're making good time.

We Have Arrived!

We got home just before the sun went down. Boogy and Patch started barking even before we were halfway across the lake. Soon, we could hear the other three dogs at the cabin barking back. Then I could see smoke coming out of the stovepipe of our cabin by the lake. It was good to be home!

As soon as Tehteh came in after tying the dogs to their doghouses, Mama stopped and said, "John, you look exactly like you did the day I first saw you!" Tehteh laughed and said, "You always look as pretty as the day I first saw you." Eli made a *whee-weo* whistle at their flirting and we all laughed.

Mama opened the two boxes we brought back. Tehteh pulled out a doll with a very pretty yellow dress and a matching bonnet for Nina. Eli practically squealed with joy when he got a harmonica, and Mama was speechless when she unfolded a very beautiful royal blue dress, trimmed with lace and ribbons. I got a stack of four hard-covered, real notebooks and a package of pencils! When the box was empty, Mama asked if Tehteh got anything for himself. He pulled his shirt open and revealed a brand-new pair of white long johns! "Two pairs!" he said.

The other box had brown sugar, syrup, cocoa powder, molasses and other cooking treats. I watched from my bed, smiling, as Mama, Nina and Eli crowded around the kitchen table.

The quiet scene was suddenly split by the high-pitched screech of Eli blowing and sucking on the harmonica!! Tehteh was just untying his moccasins when Mama turned to glare at him. He quickly jumped to his feet and ushered Eli out the door with him.

While Mama was dishing out the evening meal, I decided to teach Nina how to do the Charleston — one foot kicking out and then the other, with our arms swinging back and forth. But then I heard a bang and a gush of water — I had accidentally kicked the slop pail over!

*Wong Joe-on leaves his mother in China to join his father
— a man he's never met — in Canada. He can't
understand why his father would not have settled
in Vancouver's busy Chinese community, but instead runs
a makeshift café in a small Saskatchewan town.*

PAUL YEE *was born in Saskatchewan, but moved
to Vancouver at a young age. While he was growing up,
no books about the Chinese in Canada were available,
so he set out to create them himself.*

Prairie Showdown

✍

The Diary of Wong Joe-on

Tybalt, Saskatchewan
August – October 1921

[Translated from Chinese]

August 25, 1921

It is the day's end so I congratulate myself. Why? Because no one else will.

Well done, Wong Joe-on, very well done, to travel alone for twenty-two days, across the world's biggest ocean and two and a half Canadian provinces! Yes, Uncle Chung escorted me, but only to Vancouver. Not once did I fall sick, lose my way, or get in trouble!

Unfortunately, trouble began when I reached Tybalt. I had been so eager to meet my father. Then I gave up on him.

At the train station, Ba snapped, "Just one suitcase?"

No smile, no welcome, no thanking the gods for my safe arrival. Did he not have good feelings about my coming to Canada? Should I have stayed in China instead?

On our way to the restaurant, I tripped and fell. I wanted Ba to laugh. Instead, he grunted that this was the week's busiest day and hurried ahead. The town looked so small and empty that I doubted he could have many customers.

Ba loudly greeted his handful of patrons as they muttered among themselves. Big and burly men, they wore boots, dusty pants and sun-darkened faces. To my surprise, Ba had left them sitting in the café when he went to fetch me. Ba has no helpers, no waiters, cooks or errand boys. Did the customers not steal from him? They paid me no attention, as if Ba hadn't told them who I was. Perhaps Ba was ashamed to admit that never before had he seen his thirteen-year-old son.

The "restaurant" is a pitiful wooden shack. It is hardly worthy of the name café. Splinters defend its walls. Floor planks are uneven. Oilcloths lay over tables and a counter. Seats are wooden crates and fancy-back chairs. I smelled burnt meat and stale grease. The worst horse stable in China is better furnished than this "King's Café." No royalty would ever set foot here!

Ba told me to wash dishes and chop kindling. But I kept peeking out front, wanting to see faces, hear English and learn my job. To the back, the land rolled flat under a giant sky. Far away were hills and a few trees. There were no buildings, roads or humans — nothing for adventure or excitement.

I went to wash the front window. The heat was intense outside; the bright sun made me squint. Across the road, men surrounded an auto. I kept glancing at it. How did such Western machines travel over land without animal power or human help? Then I saw human legs jutting out from under it. I ran to see if someone was dead, but a man rudely shoved me back. Then Ba stepped in and yanked me away.

At bedtime, I presented Ma's letter and started to talk about our dikes collapsing. Ba snapped, "Did I ask you to speak?"

Ba has no right to chide me like that. I came here, across a whole ocean, to work. I should be treated like an adult!

August 29

This place is a prison. Ba views me as a toddler. When I go pump water, I return quickly, before he comes looking for me. When the restaurant emptied this afternoon, I thought to walk around town. Ba said no, it was too hot outside. He added that the Westerners dislike us and might do harm. Instead, I washed the window again.

Why come to Canada if I cannot explore it?

Dust and tumbleweeds drift by our restaurant all day long. People walk with their heads bent against the wind, hands clutching their hats. Some cars rumble by and kick up clouds of choking powder. Horse-drawn wagons leave mounds of dung that remind me of our water buffalo in China. Even our buffalo is luckier than me, because Ma and Grandma treat it lovingly.

Ba greets all his customers cheerfully. A few reply to him. Ba makes conversation. Sometimes it stops; sometimes people start to laugh. If Ba were half as friendly to me, I would be happy. I must learn English so I know what he is saying to them!

Ba scowls whenever he is in the kitchen, but out front he gives customers smiles and booming welcomes. How can I trust someone with two faces?

I joked about the heat but he snapped back, declaring that this was a farming place (as if I had not noticed). They needed hot weather to ensure crops were dry enough to harvest.

September 2

I stopped writing for a few days after my arrival, but then I decided to keep going. Only this journal keeps me from bashing my head on a wall.

I thought I had left Ma's nagging behind in China. Instead, her question plagues me like a noisy mosquito: Why does your father not come home?

The villagers gave spiteful answers: He took a wife with blue eyes. He started a second family over there. He prospered and abandoned his past.

Such talk left Ma weeping.

I see nothing here to warrant such talk. Instead, I see reasons for Ba to leave. His customers are rude. To summon him, they thump their cups or rattle their plates. One man left without paying yesterday. Ba refused to let me chase him. Another man slammed down coins but kicked over our best chair.

Ba works longer than our farmers at harvest. At dawn when he wakes me, bread and pies are already in the oven. He cooks, greets customers, fetches ice and orders supplies. We close late. Ba sleeps only about five hours.

Yesterday I woke early when it was still cool, planning to sneak out for a walk. Ba was busy stacking bottles under the front window, where he had removed a section of the wall. The café is so pitifully small that every inch of space must be used for storage. I crept back to bed. China's farmers relax a bit between planting and harvesting, but I doubt Ba does that. Does he even remember how to plant rice?

Western food is either bland or overly sweet. Potatoes, carrots and peas get boiled into mush. Meat — slabs of it, not bites — is seared black as coal. Fruit is baked until watery, between thin bread. All inedible. If I wanted to starve to death, I would have stayed in China. Why didn't Ba settle in Vancouver, which has scores of Chinese restaurants? Why stay in this out-of-the-way town, with such meagre prospects?

September 5

I was peeling potatoes with a dull knife when Ba called for me. I was startled to meet a Chinese man and boy. I thought Ba and me were the only Chinese here. Uncle Guy runs the town hotel and its dining room. Sonny is eleven and short. I arrived ten days ago, yet never saw these people. That shows how caged I am.

Uncle Guy praised my height and muscles. He asked if I had been seasick and if my train had arrived on time — more than Ba had ever asked me. It felt good to speak and to be heard. Uncle Guy brought fresh-baked buns, his specialty. Sonny needs a new friend, he said.

But what use do I have for such a boy?

Hawk and I hated having his little brothers follow us everywhere. Now I miss them — no doubt they still stir up trouble each day.

Ba said tomorrow Sonny will take me to school. School? I came for work, not classes! I am not a little boy. Ba laughed and demanded if I could serve customers now. I had to say no. I only know the alphabet and some numbers. Uncle Guy said the teacher rents a room at his hotel.

Ba was guarded with Uncle Guy, not jolly as he is with customers. Later I learned that Ba opened the first restaurant in this town. Uncle Guy came later.

"I should not befriend Sonny," I said, thinking Ba would agree. "We cannot trust them."

Ba called me stupid.

If I am stupid, why should I waste my time going to school? I hate sitting for hours.

September 6

I knew nothing good would come from school. It was humiliating.

Because I spoke no English, I had to sit with the Grade Ones. Their feet dangled from the seats. My knees banged the desk. I looked to be too stupid for my proper grade. Sonny already spoke English and sat elsewhere. Everyone else is a Westerner.

Teacher is too young to know much. He pointed into a book and spoke. I repeated his sounds. The picture showed a cat chasing a mouse.

Mid-morning, everyone ran outside. I thought class was over. Sonny said it was rest time. He told me only English could be spoken at school. When I heard that some students from Europe also spoke no English, I felt better.

I went to the outhouse, and heard shouting and hooting. Two older boys were pushing Sonny back and forth. I went and marched him away, but one boy grabbed me from behind. Sonny and I told him to let go but the boy shoved me into his friend's grip. Sonny shouted again for a stop. When the first one ran at me, head down in order to butt me in the stomach, I turned and slammed my hand into his friend's face. When he yelped in pain, I planted a foot behind him and flipped him onto the ground.

Sonny's eyes widened.

At noon, he and I ran to his hotel. He told me those boys' names. I could not make them out, but they sounded like Jaw-jee and Wee-yum. We decided to tell our fathers nothing about the fight. It would only bring us trouble.

After afternoon classes, our enemies were waiting. Jaw-jee grabbed me from behind while Wee-yum shoved

Sonny down the stairs. Other students screamed and gathered to watch.

My elbows shot out. I yanked Jaw-jee's hand and jabbed my elbow into his stomach. He gasped and bent forward. My arm circled to his back and threw him to the ground.

I strolled home slowly. I had promised Master never to start a fight. I had kept my word. Sonny asked about my *kung fu,* so I told him about loudmouths back home who hounded me, like that man who doubted I had a father because he had never seen Ba's face. I didn't start those fights either, but I knew how to finish them.

All evening, whenever the café door opened, I looked up, expecting to see my enemies. What will I do if Ba forbids me from fighting?

September 7

Jaw-jee was not at school today. What a relief! Maybe he is hiding his bruises, or is afraid to face me. Not that I fear him. But we have started a battle that is unfinished. Of course Jaw-jee plans revenge. I would, if I were him.

Later that afternoon, I threw dishwater over our garden behind the café. A puff of cloud hung near the ground, far to one end of the blue horizon. When I came out again fifteen minutes later, the cloud had darkened and grown ten, fifteen times, up and down. I have never seen anything sprout so quickly. The giant cloud blackened the land beneath, and jags of lightning lashed out.

Meanwhile the other end of the horizon remained bright blue. I ran inside. What if the lightning set the crops aflame? It was too awful to imagine.

Fifteen minutes later, when I peeked again, the cloud had shrunk and drifted higher. Most of the sky was blue again. What a strange, terrifying land!

September 8

I did not fight today, even though I was provoked. Master would have praised me.

Ba served hot soup to a man and hurried away. The man had no spoon so I took one over and smiled. When I turned away, something hard bounced off my head. The spoon clattered to the floor. Ba quickly fetched another one. I had brought the wrong size. For soup, it is the bigger one. The man was not a regular customer. If he comes back, I will spit into his coffee before serving it.

September 9

Teacher ate dinner here. He ordered the roast beef.

I was surprised to see him because Uncle Guy's place is better. A soft but shiny hard sheet covers his floor. White stone tabletops sit on fancy iron legs. Uncle Guy's white shirt and tie are clean, and his apron is spotless. Ba's dark shirt has caked stains that he thinks no one can see.

Ba grinned at Teacher. I listened to them talk but understood nothing. Later Ba called Teacher a smart man because he eats here one day and at Uncle Guy's the next to avoid offending anyone.

Ba did not shout at me, so I think Teacher did not mention my schoolyard fight. I wondered when Jaw-jee might return to school, but dared not ask Ba to translate.

September 10

No school today. Ba asked if there was homework. I said no. Ba threatened to ask Teacher himself.

For the first time, I saw a woman and children here. Town children never come into Ba's café, although they yank open our door and scream insults before fleeing and laughing.

The woman had thin, pinched cheeks. Her dress was limp from too much washing, and her shoes hung loose on her feet. But the children were plump, with healthy faces and store-bought clothes. The girls' braids were tied with red ribbons. Along with a brother, the girls ate apple pie as the woman leaned back and closed her eyes. She was exhausted. Ba gave her many cups of coffee. She nodded gratefully each time. I guessed she was a farmer's wife. Such women work very hard.

She made me think about the women who live in town. When I pass them, they stiffen and inch away, as if I carry a strange disease. But this farmer woman smiled at me when I took away her empty dishes.

September 11

Rage is boiling inside me. Jaw-jee took revenge today, but not just against me. He attacked Ba and our café. I never mentioned my fight with Jaw-jee, so even now, Ba blames the damage on Westerners' disrespect.

Jaw-jee rode a *horse* into our café! It shrieked and reared up, kicking its front legs. Its head smashed the ceiling while its eyelids spread wide and its eye-whites flashed madly. Tables and chairs fell over. Food and drink crashed. Our customers fled. One kick could kill any man.

Shouting foul names, Jaw-jee made his horse chase Ba, but Ba stood his ground at the window. He yelled and waved his apron at the horse. Several times, Jaw-jee charged at Ba and shouted at him to get out and get out of town, but Ba wouldn't leave his spot. I ran to pull Ba outside and let the horse follow us, but Ba shook me off. I screamed when the horse bucked wildly over us, but Ba was determined to guard the bottles he had put into the wall. I swung a chair at Jaw-jee, but Ba stopped me. Finally the horse galloped back out the door.

Ba cursed him in Chinese. I trembled from fear and anger. Meals were left unpaid. The horse had dented the floor. I shuddered to imagine such cracks in a human skull.

September 12

Jaw-jee was at school, talking loudly at the back. I braced myself to fight. At recess, Teacher kept Jaw-jee and Wee-yum inside. Then, at lunch, Teacher stopped

Sonny and me. He spoke to Sonny, who told me in Chinese to stop fighting Jaw-jee. I should consider the feud "even" because I had beaten Jaw-jee twice. I told Sonny to say that Jaw-jee had caused more damage than me. Teacher said that if I stopped fighting, then he would not mention the schoolyard fight to Ba. How did Teacher know I had not told Ba? Did Sonny tell? I must learn English quickly!

At day's end, students gathered around Jaw-jee and Wee-yum in the yard. When Sonny and I came out, someone shouted and they all laughed. Sometimes it is best not to understand English.

September 15

Ba finally lets me serve food. Before, he said no, that I would drop the plates, and that customers resented a child waiter.

Now he tells me where the order goes: window table, door table, tiny table or slanted table. If the customer sits among others at the counter, then Ba says who: four-eyes, hat-and-tie, train master or police officer. So far, no armed soldiers like the squads of scowling men with rifles who harass the markets in China. And Ba names each dish aloud so I can call it out at the table. I hope to count money or to cook soon.

Jaw-jee comes to school one day but not the next. I never know if he will be there but I do not worry. I fight better.

September 19

Teacher saw that I truly knew my alphabet, big letters and small, from learning them in China. Now I copy words where one letter connects to another in a single thread. The letters change shape, so it is hard work. Still, it sets me apart from the Grade Ones, so I want to learn quickly. Ba likes it when I do homework. He chants a proverb: *Books and pages contain gold and jade.* He should let me work quietly.

I promised to write to Ma but have not done so. I feel bad, because she will worry if she has no letter from me.

September 22

Two policemen walked in today. Our customers knew them. Ba greeted the officers with smiles and brave words, and called for two cups of coffee. When I delivered, one officer gravely shook my hand and spoke English to me. Ba said in Chinese to smile and say hello. As the three men laughed, Ba added while grinning widely that I must go and empty the white teapot into the outhouse.

I thought it strange because we ate and drank every bit of leftover. At the outhouse, I sniffed the teapot. Liquor. But why such a fuss? Teahouses at home served it.

In the kitchen, the officers peered into shelves and pulled out pots and sacks. They found sealed bottles and wanted them opened. Ba protested. They insisted. They sniffed and frowned. As they stomped out, Ba hurried after them. Then I took a sniff. It was vinegar!

Later Ba explained that the government wanted to stop Canadians from drinking liquor and had banned stores and eating places from selling it. But people craved their liquor, so many businessmen sold it illegally. Ba was breaking the law! Then I realized why Ba had put bottles in that hidden section of the wall. Luckily, the police cannot read Chinese. They could have learned Ba's secret from this journal!

Tonight Ba trusted me with an important secret. I am an adult.

September 24

I cannot stop thinking about liquor. When Teacher drinks from a bottle, or when Uncle Guy fills his customers' glasses, I wonder if it is really water. When Ba sent me to the store to buy fruit spices, I saw shelves of bottles. I wanted to ask if the police sniffed them. Ma and Grandma dislike men who drink too much. Me, I wonder how men enjoy something that tastes so awful.

September 26

The worst part of school is singing. The little ones chirp along happily in their high voices, but my voice is deeper. Even I know we sound terrible. Reading aloud together is all right, because there are no high notes.

Each day, class starts with a song. The older children

know it while we new students are learning by hearing it over and over. Sonny said we are asking God to protect our king. But I thought Canada had democracy, not a king. Now I see how Ba chose the name for his café!

I wait eagerly for class to end. If I took my journal to class, I would write much more, in Chinese. But Teacher would take it away.

September 28

I finally saw Canada! This morning, we were dismissed from school because Teacher went to help with the harvest. Sonny and I shared glances as we passed the gate of the schoolyard. Without a word, we headed out of town. Who cared about our fathers?

Freedom! I was so glad, it did not matter that there was little to see. The town shrank behind us. Ahead lay miles of flat land, some filled with a light yellow crop, others by a darker gold. Our footsteps crunched over the dry road, as insects darted to and fro.

Sonny ran ahead, hollering to the sky. He started spinning, around and around, faster and faster until he fell. He got up laughing. I was too old to play but could not resist Sonny's cheer. We spun in circles. We ran with arms out, like hawks circling high above. We cawed and screeched like birds, sprinting until we needed air.

Black smoke rose. We saw some men at a great iron barrel that belched dark smoke. Sacks of coal were waiting to be burned. A long belt connected the iron barrel to a noisy machine where men pitched in grain at one end. Straw flew out from the other end. Horse-drawn machines combed the fields, cutting the crop while wagons waited to take away the grain. Women came to bring something, probably food, to the men. Drivers waved at us; I suppose they were too far to see we were Chinese.

Sonny ran after a butterfly. A car puttered behind us. I stepped aside to let it pass, but it pulled up beside Sonny, who shouted for me and jumped into the car. In an instant we were roaring along the fields. Bouncing up and down, I clutched at the seat and the door, thrilled at my first ride. Sonny saw my big grin and nudged the driver, who chuckled and gave me a thumbs-up. They laughed and chattered, shouting over the rush of air. We went so fast that I thought I was flying!

Harvested fields held stumps of dry stalks in prickly rows. At another field, men swung a tool with long sharp fingers to cut grain. Little boys and girls collected stalks and lugged buckets, going from one chore to another. I should have offered to help Teacher with the harvest.

In town, a horse and rider darted into our path without warning. Our car screeched to a halt, and our driver bellowed furiously. When the rider peered into the car, we saw Jaw-jee. He made an angry arm gesture at us and shouted at the driver before galloping away.

After we got out, Sonny was surprised that I did not know our driver was the liquor delivery man. In return, I realized that Uncle Guy does sell liquor. He owns such a high-class place. Sonny bragged about his father's hiding place for liquor, and I told him about Ba's.

I expected Ba to scold me, but he was preoccupied, He was puzzled because Jaw-jee's father had ordered him to come to apologize for riding the horse through the café. I mentioned how our driver had almost crashed into Jaw-jee. Ba ordered me never to wander off again without telling him first.

October 5

The harvest is finished and Jaw-jee came back to school. The harvest inspired Teacher to make us work with our hands. We were given long thin strips of paper and told to weave them into a mat. When I showed my little weaving to Ba, he snorted at our waste of time. Maybe if we do more silly things in class, then Ba will let me quit school.

October 8

Trust no one.

Today the police burst in, marched straight to the front window and removed the wall beneath it. They found the liquor and arrested Ba. Our customers fled even though I chased them for money.

It had to be Sonny who told our secret. I ran to the hotel and grabbed him. I slapped and punched him. He didn't know how to defend himself. Uncle Guy came running and pulled me away. I wanted to hit out and kick him too, but he held me firmly at arm's length. He pretended to know nothing, so I confronted him. Did

Sonny tell him where Ba hid his liquor? Had Uncle Guy told the police? Uncle Guy said I was talking nonsense and flung me away.

Of course they were guilty. How else could the police go right to our hiding place?

I noticed our customers strolling into Uncle Guy's place. That was why he had betrayed us — to grab our customers on the busiest day of the week!

I locked our front door and fixed the broken wall with nails and boards. I stored the meat Ba had been cooking. All day, people banged the door. I guessed at how much money we were losing. It was all my fault.

Will Ba be jailed? It could be for weeks or months! Could I run the café myself? How could I find Ba? Teacher might help me, but I needed Sonny or Uncle Guy to talk to him. What a disaster. If I went home to China now, I would be the biggest laughingstock in the county.

October 9

This morning I started the fire and boiled water. There was bread and pie from yesterday. Many times I had watched Ba cook breakfast. I set out butter and jam. When a customer entered, I shouted good morning and poured coffee. I listened carefully for "ham" or "bacon" and then fried meat and eggs, and made toast. I let the customers talk. I made a second breakfast, a third and then a fourth. When I collected my first twenty cents, I almost floated into the sky.

Mid-morning, Ba came back. He said nothing about the police. We worked madly to catch up. I stirred the jelly. Ba baked, cut meat for lunch and dinner, and made soup. I pared potatoes, sliced tomatoes and shelled peas. Ba gruffly said that I had done well to serve breakfast.

But I fretted how to admit that I was the one who told Sonny about Ba's hiding place.

Finally, all customers were gone and our workday was finished. I washed dishes while Ba prepared for tomorrow. I told him about Sonny, and urged him to take revenge by telling the police where Uncle Guy hid his liquor.

To my surprise, Ba insisted that Uncle Guy had not informed on him. I said that Uncle Guy must have, because how else did the police know where to go? Ba raised Jaw-jee's name. Had he not seen me in the liquor car? Had he not seen Ba protecting the window wall from the horse? Ba also mentioned that last week the police stopped the bootlegger's car and questioned him. Jaw-jee and his father happened to be in town and saw it.

"Don't think that Jaw-jee is stupid," Ba said. "He is smart too."

I fell quiet. I never thought of that. What a stupid ass I was.

I went to sweep the floor, but Ba handed me a slab of meat and some vegetables, and told me to make tomorrow's lunch. He took pen and paper to the front counter.

I had watched Ba cook pot roast many times, so I seared the beef in hot oil and then browned the chopped-up onions and carrots. I added soup-water, salt and pepper, and dried green spices, and let it simmer.

Ba didn't come watch me, so he must trust me now. He had never imagined I could cook and serve breakfasts on my own, had he?

When he strolled past me, heading to the outhouse, I sneaked out front.

He was finally writing a letter to Ma! He mentioned my safe arrival and said he was pleased with my good health and intelligence, which let me provide great help to him.

Why doesn't he say this to my face?

Ba also explained his long absence from China. He had started several cafés but in one town, a rival left him bankrupt. In another town, a fire burned him out. He left a third town because its residents bullied him. However, Uncle Guy had lent him money each time to start again.

So that's why Ba says Uncle Guy has not betrayed us!

At the end, Ba asked Ma to forgive him for being too ashamed to admit his failures.

When Ba came in the back door, I grabbed the broom and hurried out to the sidewalk to hide my tears.

I still do not fully understand Ba, but now I respect him.

After World War II, many Jewish families immigrated
to North America and a few were able to get into Canada.
Many were broken from the struggle to survive the war.
They still grieved the loss of their dear ones who had died
in ghettoes and concentration camps, and some were
trying to find other lost members of their families.

LILLIAN BORAKS-NEMETZ is herself a survivor of
the Warsaw ghetto. She has written about the war years
in her novel, The Old Brown Suitcase.

In the Silence of My Heart

❧
The Diary of Miriam Hartfeld

Montreal, Quebec
June – September 1947

June 10ᵗʰ, 1947, evening

This afternoon when I opened my school bag something blue fell out. Lo and behold, it was a little leatherbound book with a key and *Diary* written on the cover in gold letters, and inside only blank pages with lines on them. Don't understand how it got there. No one has access to my school bag, and my parents would not go there. I wonder if I should be wicked and take a chance on writing something in it, but what?

And what if someone finds out all about my secret life? Nobody seems very interested, except Abe and Deborah. It's good to have new friends — Abe helping me with things I don't understand in school, and Deborah being my example of a Canadian girl much more grown up than I, though we're the same age.

In any case, I have decided to write about my birthday.

Happy Birthday to me!!!!

I am Miriam Hartfeld, an immigrant from Warsaw, Poland. I was born on June 10th, 1934.

I am Jewish.

How good it is to be able to say this — to say my real name — after six years of hiding in a Polish village, with a false identity paper that said I was Zosia Bielska, a Catholic whose parents died when Nazis attacked Poland in 1939. Lies of course. But Papa said we must do what we need to survive.

It's safe here in Canada, even though Papa said they didn't want to take in Jewish people after the war. Thank goodness Uncle Bronek came here long enough ago and was able to sponsor us. And now here we are in Montreal, Quebec, and I love the French language. Sometimes, even better than English.

It has already been half a year since Mama, Papa, Georgie and I arrived in the Port of Halifax last January. I cannot believe that we came without Katya, but how do you find a sister who simply disappeared during the war, even though we looked for her everywhere. I miss her so. She is still my best friend, even if she is six years older than I.

It was awful to be put into Grade Seven and then fail all the tests. I sat in that classroom like a dummy. But at least when my English improved I started doing better after studying very hard.

A confession:

I started writing this first entry in Polish, then translated it into English. It "killed" me (as they say here) to see how the translation made it possible to substitute words from one language to another. Seeing Polish changing into English, and meaning the same, made me feel friendlier towards the English language. It kind of broke the barrier between my two cultures. Of course, I used a dictionary a lot, and a grammar book. And it puzzles me the way English is used. For instance "to kill," which can mean "to murder," can also mean "to amaze or overwhelm." "Kill" is after all a serious word.

My English is still in its infant stages and has only just begun to crawl — like my brother Georgie did a few months ago.

Mama and Papa went out early today and left a note wishing me a Happy Birthday. They also left a package, and in it a practical gift of panties and socks. I felt a bit disappointed not to have received the red purse they knew I so wanted to carry on weekends. Deborah has a purse and so do the other girls at school. My parents think that a girl my age only needs a wallet. Surely a thirteen-year-old is old enough to carry a purse? Mama and Papa are so old-fashioned. In Poland, girls my age are not allowed to wear lipstick, let alone carry a handbag or, G-d forbid, wear shoes with little heels. I tell Mama and Papa that this is 1947 in Canada, and thirteen-year-old girls are so much more sophisticated. But they don't listen.

I know that we don't have money for what my parents call "frills." Not just yet, that is. Papa is studying English and promises to get a good job next year. It doesn't seem to matter here that he was a doctor in

Poland. He has to pass medical exams all over again. In the meantime I know he does his best as a part-time helper at a local clinic, while Mama works for a friend in a small boutique.

I hate having to babysit Georgie after school — a very boring occupation. Days seem bland with nothing much to look forward to. But miracles do happen, like finding this diary.

I enjoy being able to say things here that I couldn't otherwise talk about. Like my personal stuff . . . Besides, Mama and Papa frown at some of my ideas, like my wanting to look older than thirteen. If only Katya were here.

Maybe I could write to *her* in my diary? I would tell her everything and it would be safe because I can lock the diary. Besides, it seems silly to just write in a blank book without a living soul reading or hearing what I have to say. Yet I wouldn't want others to know my innermost feelings, especially Mama and Papa — they wouldn't understand.

I shouldn't be so mean. After all, they made a special supper for me and invited Debbie and then sang "*Sto Lat*" to wish that I live a hundred years. After we devoured that delicious chocolate cake, I started talking about the war. Papa told me to keep quiet and never to mention that subject again. To forget Polish, the war, the Holocaust and everything I remember about my country, and to start living a Canadian life, in English. Then they went back to their English grammar books while I played with Georgie and later cried myself to sleep. I didn't —

I don't — want to forget all those things and I never will. Never. And that is a part of my big secret. The other part I can't even think about now.

Here in my diary I can remember whatever I want to, in whatever language I wish.

Later

I should give my diary a name, as if I were speaking to someone with a name. But not just any name.

After much mulling over I have decided to call the diary Kati, and talk to you, my precious sister. Of course the word Sis doesn't make sense in Polish, but in English everything is abbreviated anyhow. And I have to start somewhere in this difficult language.

June 11ᵗʰ, 1947

Dear Kati,

I just had the most horrible dream. There was a sound of marching feet, banging on the door, then . . .

No . . . It's too unbearable to write about now!

June 15ᵗʰ, 1947

Dear Kati,

Maybe if I tell my dream to you, I can manage to put it all down:

I hear a sound of feet marching down the hall. Someone bangs on the door. The knob turns and a man in the black uniform of Hitler's SS police force stomps in. He comes closer. I can only see his eye. The soldiers are mean and they are

*coming closer and closer to my face till I can't breathe. I am
so scared. I know he is going to hurt me. I want to scream but
no sound comes from my throat.*

The night of the dream, I woke up all sweaty. I
couldn't even write most of the dream. But now that I've
told you, I feel a little better.

Nightmares like this have happened before too.

This is why I cannot forget, Kati:

I feel as if I have an album of pictures in my head
that opens every so often and I can see photographs of
the war, the soldiers, guns, people running. . . . Our poor
granny, who got left behind in Poland all alone. . . . Papa
saying we couldn't take her along because we only had
visas for the four of us. . . . Grandpa getting beaten by a
Nazi soldier on a ghetto street. . . . And I still remember
afterwards how he lay in his bed, very ill, in that dark
and shabby room, smelling of mold and garlic, with yellow teeth swimming in a big dirty glass. . . . Papa coming
home with tears in his eyes and telling us that Grandpa
was gone — that Nazis had no use for the old folk.

I don't remember crying, Kati. When I think back, I
realize that I was in shock, and still am.

I also have in my mind-album (that is what I call it)
pictures of all our aunts, uncles and cousins who died in
the concentration camp. How they were sent to the
horrible Umschlagplatz in the ghetto to be loaded onto
the waiting cattle cars and on to that camp called
Treblinka, never to be heard from again. But I will
always remember them. Alla, who drew portraits of

people, was the oldest of us all. Remember how she would often stand in front of the mirror, looking at herself, fixing her hair for hours because she wanted to look nice for the boy down the hall? It was hard, she said, when she only owned one soiled polka-dot dress. And Irena, who wrote beautiful poems and wanted to be just like her older sister and also look nice for the same boy.

And remember our two boy cousins, one wanting to be a doctor and the other an inventor? Adam would put unlikely things together to create other unlikely things. They were so serious for their years and were always reading a lot. And our three aunts simply vanishing one day. Remember how they were all musical and good-looking with their dark hair and eyes? Now here we are with only the four of us left, plus Uncle Bronek, out of our whole big family.

I also have a photograph of you, Kati. A beautiful young girl with dark wavy hair and big brown eyes that were full of tears the day you escaped the ghetto to the other side of the wall. I cried and cried after you left to live with that family in the village. You never knew that I went later to another place, and I survived. But you got lost, Mama said.

I always feel guilty when Mama looks at me with her sad blue eyes, as if I were supposed to be you. That is when I want to run away or shrink into myself and never come out.

Bye for now, my Kati.

Love, Miriam

June 30th, 1947

Dear Kati,

I wish these were letters I could send you so you could answer back, but I don't know where you are. I will read each one out loud and imagine that wherever you may be, you can hear me.

Since the day you disappeared from our lives, our family has not been the same. Mama and Papa changed so much around that time. Of course, many people's lives were broken by the war, parts of which I can still remember. Like the day in Warsaw when I was supposed to help you pack for your escape from the ghetto, but instead I went to play in the courtyard with the little boy next door. When I came back inside, you were gone and I have never seen you since. That little boy got typhus and died the very next week. Then the Germans invaded our quarter and we were sent to the deportation depot. Father had a friend who was able to get us into the hospital there and through the back door into a truck that got us back into the ghetto. As we drove out in the covered truck, I peered through the little opening and saw German soldiers pointing their guns at our truck while there we sat behind the tarpaulin. I thought they'd kill us any minute, but they didn't shoot.

You don't know any of this, Kati. You don't know how I eventually got out of the ghetto. It was scary, as the Germans were ordered to shoot anyone who tried to escape. I was taken out by a Christian lady who did these things to help save Jewish children. She pretended I was her niece and took me out through the courthouse. Of course you had to be blond with green eyes, as I was, and have false papers saying you were a Catholic. Dark-haired people were stereotyped as Jews and had to hide. With your dark hair and dark eyes, I shudder to think what might have happened to you on the Aryan side. The Aryan side — that's what they called the non-Jewish side of Warsaw, on the other side of the big wall that enclosed us Jews. The worst part was saying good-bye to Mama and Papa. I became someone else that day — a Catholic child whose name was Zosia Bielska. I am not sure that I am Miriam again even now.

I keep on asking Mama why we left without knowing what happened to you. But all she does is shake her head and cry, saying, "We couldn't help it" or "I don't know." This makes me mad. If it were up to me I would have never left without knowing where you were. Someday, Kati, when I am older, I vow to return to Poland to look for you.

You will see that I can keep my word.
Love, Miriam

August 5th, 1947

Dear Kati,

Where have I been? I have not written for so long because many things have happened. I was lost between English and Polish in a non-language world. I hated English words, with so many words having double or triple meanings, and fought it with all my might, hanging onto my native language. Before school's end, the teacher noticed my struggle and said that when two beasts fight over their prey, the third gets it.

I am finally living and writing in English — well, almost. As a result, Deborah and I have grown closer. I got some money for babysitting Georgie and was able to buy that red purse I wanted. A secret, Kati: In it I kept a pink lipstick, which I put on at school and took off before I got home. One day I forgot to wipe it off and I was called into our living room for a family conference.

I sat there, in front of them (my parental judges) while they were angrily asking me questions about the lipstick. I told them Deborah put it on me in school. In the meantime Georgie dragged off my purse and smeared the lipstick all over the dresser mirror in my room, squealing with delight. Mama and Papa stampeded into my room, and Papa hit me for lying. Parents shouldn't frighten their children into lying. I was simply too scared to tell them the truth. Now whose fault is that?

Of course, they have been under a terrible strain, and Papa has been very upset, and lately it seems to be even worse. He never hit either of us before, do you agree? He later told me that he was sorry, and his hand shook when he stroked the place he hit me.

Despite Papa's apology, sometimes I dislike our parents. How can I ever forgive Papa for this?
Love, Miriam

August 10th, 1947

Dear Kati,

The other part of my secret, besides the mind-album and the lipstick, is the boy I met at a school dance. His name is Abe — short for Abraham, like the father of our ancestors. Did you know? It's in the Old Testament and I learned about it from Deborah, because she heard various stories from her father, so she knows the history of our people. You must have known that during the war, we had to hide our Jewishness when outside the ghetto. But here it is all over the place. It's in the delis, in the barrels of pickles and containers of chopped herring. In the Star of David (King of the Jews) painted on the shop windows, and men in black coats, hats and locks hanging beneath.

The last time I saw a Jewish star was in the ghetto, when adults had to wear arm bands with Stars of David to identify them as Jews. Here you don't need any of that and all the Jewish people proudly strut the main street as if it belonged to them — and you know what? It does. It is different here, freer and more peaceful. The only siren comes from a fire engine, not an air raid. Abe really helped me to feel that I belong too, though I don't as yet. And so did Deb. She made me a gift of my first bra, which mother said I didn't need, and Abe kissed me in a school hallway when no one was looking. Papa would kill me if he knew.

I really like Abe, but Papa would have a fit if he knew about this boy and that I liked it when he kissed me.

Here is another thing. Having a fit can mean becoming very angry, or having an epileptic fit, which means a very bad thing for your health, and it can also mean to fit well into your clothes. The English language can be so complicated. Anyway Papa did have a fit — the angry kind.

Love, Miriam

September 4th, 1947

Dear Kati,

I hardly see our parents. All I do is slave over English and French, and babysit Georgie. He is a little monster to look after. One day I invited Abe to babysit with me, and for some reason that day Papa came home earlier than usual. You should have seen what happened. I want to disappear when I think of it.

Papa's face went green when he saw Abe. He rushed up towards him with hateful eyes and asked in a rasping voice, "Who are you, sir?" I almost thought if he had a weapon, he would have killed him.

Abe stood tall and motionless. Papa jumped up at him with two clenched fists aimed at Abe's jaw. When Abe ducked and Papa fell over the dining-room table, I wanted to laugh and to cry. Part of me thought, Good for Abe. The other thought, Poor Papa — as he scrambled off the table and told Abe to get out.

Abe said goodbye to me and quietly left.

Papa pushed me onto a dining-room chair and shouted questions without even giving me a chance to answer. When I weakly replied that Abe was simply helping me to look after Georgie — which was the holy truth — Papa went green again and slapped my face on both sides till I thought I'd go deaf. I did see stars before my eyes, Kati. Just then Georgie started to shriek and Papa turned towards me, his face all contorted as if he were in pain, and said in a muffled tone of voice, "I am so sorry, Miri. I didn't mean to hit you. I am only trying to protect you." Then he turned towards the window.

I accepted his apology matter-of-factly, but I am honestly not sure what Papa was protecting me from. In the meantime I really started to appreciate Georgie. After all, his scream helped bring Papa back to himself.

When Mama came home she didn't seem to care about what had happened, and I felt very lonely. As you yourself know, in Poland a girl my age could not be seen walking along with a boy. Papa was being protective of me. But don't you think he overdid it this time?

Deborah has a boyfriend. His name is Jacob and her parents don't seem to mind if they chum around. But they are Canadians. It's more progressive here. After all, kids our age only go out in groups to movies, or school dances that are chaperoned.

As for more excitement, today a mysterious letter arrived from Poland.

I found it when I came home from school. It was addressed to Papa, and the return address was from a Mr. Gertner, a lawyer friend of Papa's.

It was in an airmail envelope, well-sealed, and I daren't have opened it. Someone said that if you wave it in front of a steaming kettle it will unseal the envelope, but I daren't. This is the first letter from Poland since we left.

Love, Miriam

September 10th, 1947

Dear Kati,

Something has happened. Last night I heard Mama and Papa talking in whispers and I thought I heard someone crying. When I tried to walk into the kitchen they told me to go to my room. Papa was holding the letter I mentioned. I still wonder what's in it.

September 11th, 1947

I couldn't sleep. They talked all night long. This morning Mama had red eyes and Papa looked miserable. I didn't know if this was about me, or something else. I felt as if I had done something wrong.

School today seemed endless and I felt blah. Even Abe couldn't make me feel better, though he bought me an ice cream cone at recess from a little white truck with music. Deborah asked what was wrong, but all I could do was say I didn't know. How lucky I am to have such good and caring friends.

In the afternoon I went home, burning to find out what was going on.

Until later,

Love, Miriam

September 12ᵗʰ, 1947

There is still the problem of that letter. I tried to sneak into their bedroom and I looked for it everywhere, but it was nowhere to be found. Our parents never talk to me anymore, Kati. They have become strangers even more. This made me realize that I really don't know them anymore as my parents.

After the Warsaw ghetto they struggled so hard to survive, running from one barn to another, and afterwards hiding in cold wintry forests so Nazis wouldn't catch them. Of course I didn't see them for several years — just as you did not — and then when they came back and told me that you were missing, they were already changed. They looked tired, worn and shabby. I can still see the tears in their eyes. Our father, who had always been well-dressed, and our mother, who had a beautiful face and figure and wore the most stylish clothes before the war (from what little I can remember of those times) — those parents were no more. They looked afraid, more like beggars on the poorer streets of Warsaw. And they were hungry. The old woman in the house where I lived wouldn't even let me hug them when they came to visit me, because the neighbours might notice and think I was their daughter. We could not risk the truth.

When I saw what they looked like, I felt afraid to ask them questions. And there was so much I wanted to know about what happened to you. That day, and on other days and nights, I sensed danger all around me. The old woman told me that if I were found out to be a Jewish child, I would be killed.

Here in Montreal, Mama hasn't really spoken to me much, except to say do this and do that. And Papa is always busy and frowning. When I say something, he simply ignores me, save to remind me to do my homework, and shout when I do one little thing that is more Canadian than Polish — and yet they want me to become a Canadian quickly.

Often, I feel like running away. Deborah said I could stay with her. Abe said I should try to tell our parents that I would like them to treat me the way they used to when they loved me. How do I do that? I feel they don't love me anymore and only need me for babysitting Georgie, which has become a chore, with me always wishing he were you, Kati.

I try to forget these awful things now, but this mysterious letter has me curious and afraid. I feel I must find it, to help me understand our parents' strange behaviour.

I'll keep you posted.

Love, Miriam

September 15th, 1947

My dear Sister,

I found the letter and read it. I am copying it onto the pages of the diary, because if I don't I will never be able to face the truth.

I cannot believe what is written here. I only want to believe that by some miracle, you are somewhere listening to me . . .

Dear Jan,

I will come straight to the point.

I have investigated your daughter's disappearance and came up with following facts.

I am afraid, my dear friend, that your daughter, Katya, is no longer with us.

After someone informed on her, the Gestapo came to the house next door to inquire about her. She slipped through the back door and away from the people who were hiding her. She ran into the forest, where she joined a group of Polish Partisan fighters. They took her in, gave her a gun and even at her young age, she was shooting at the enemy. After a few of their attacks on Nazi spies in the village, the partisans were found and shot by Nazi soldiers.

Your daughter died honourably defending not only the people of Poland but fighting the cause of the poor persecuted Jews.

I am sorry to have been the one to tell you this. If you ever come back to Poland, the members of that group are buried in the village cemetery where Katya lived with the people who generously offered to hide her.

My dearest Kati, I am numb. It's as if I stopped being. When I read what the letter was saying, a terrible feeling seized me, as if a heavy shroud was settling over me. I cannot imagine what happened to you and how you must have felt — so threatened by the enemy. My dream of ever seeing you again has died, but not my dream of remembering you as you were, my beloved sister and friend.

For that, I have your photo in my mind-album, safely tucked away in the corner of my soul. From there I will always think of you. Now more than ever I need to keep on writing to you in hope that I can hear your spirit whispering in the silence of my heart.

One day I will write about you and me and all of us, for the world to know what people suffered and are still suffering, so that children and young people will never again stand in the line of fire between two countries.

I cannot write any more, my beloved sister.

Always yours,

Miriam

Growing up in the Gatineau Hills, **BRIAN DOYLE** listened
to his father and his father's friends telling tall tales
and stories. It was the Depression, then World War II,
then the years after the war when fears of the atomic bomb
loomed large. Many of Brian's novels are set in and around
Ottawa in the time of his own boyhood.

Brian enjoys stories that let the reader figure out what's
between the lines. "The world we encounter doesn't give
itself up to us all at once," he has said. And not all arrivals
are geographical — they can play out on an inner
landscape as well . . .

Entrance Certificate

∾

Penman's Journal

Ottawa, Ontario
July 1948

July 1st, 1948
Building No. 14
Unit Two
Uplands Emergency Housing Shelter
Uplands Airport Barracks
Ottawa, Ontario

Dear Dad:

The other night I heard Mom and Phil in the bedroom having a big fight and breaking the alarm clock against the door and swearing and yelling about you.

I felt like going in the bedroom with a chair and smashing Phil's face, but I couldn't because I'm afraid of him.

Then yesterday I saw Mom writing at the kitchen table. When she heard me come in she hid the paper under a placemat. Then she tried to get rid of me, telling me she wanted me to go across the parade square to the canteen to get some milk and eggs. Just then someone came to the back door and told Mom there was a phone call for her and when she went out in the hall to the pay phone I peeked at the letter. It was to you. I couldn't read much of it because Mom was coming right back, but I saw your address written on the back of an envelope so I stuck it in my pocket. Mom saw me and started to cry.

When she was done crying she made me show it to her and said I should copy it down and write you a letter.

So that's what I'm doing now, obviously.

But I don't know what to say.

She said I should tell you how I am and what I'm doing.

I'm fine.

I'm not doing much.

I was planning on telling you that I don't remember what you look like, except for some old photographs from before the war.

When I want to think about your face, I look in the mirror. They say you look like me. Or I look like you — which ever way it goes.

When I look at my bare feet they remind me of Mom's feet. When I go swimming down at the sand pits I look at my bare feet in the sand and think of Mom.

When I look at the mirror and see my face, I think I'm thinking of you.

I'm trying to figure out how many years . . .

You probably know this but I'll be fourteen this coming August.

You probably know this too, but you always forget my birthday.

This letter is not going very well.

That is about it.
I'm usually a better letter writer than this.
signed, Penman

P.S. I just thought of something. Do you love me?
signed, Penman

P.P.S. I just got an idea. I'll send you some of my journal.
Maybe it will tell you how I am and what I'm doing in this
(like my English teacher always says) the Year of Our Lord
Nineteen Hundred and Forty-Eight.
signed, Penman

SOME OF MY JOURNAL

Before Christmas holidays my teacher, Mr. Ketcheson, said that if I didn't try harder and be more "scholarly" I was going to fail English. And if I failed I wouldn't get my "Entrance Certificate" and I wouldn't be able to go to high school and then university and be a big success in life like a doctor or an engineer or something.

And that I would be a bum all my life and end up in reform school or even jail and have as my best friends extortionists and axe murderers and end up being hanged by the neck until I am dead.

Or wind up charged with committing forgery like I did with Sibyl Vane's absentee note.

Sibyl bummed school one afternoon and went to a

show at the Rathole with a guy who goes to high school and is a big-time basketball star called Stretch "The King" King. Mr. Ketcheson says it's rude to call a nice movie theatre like the Rialto, the "Rathole." (I guess he's never been there.)

Anyway, Sibyl couldn't ask her mother to write the note so she asked me would I write the note and sign her mother's name. Why didn't she get Stretch "The King" King to write the note? Because he can hardly write his own name probably. That's what everybody says about him, anyway.

It was my English teacher's fault that I wrote the note in the first place, because of a big speech he always gives us about writing. The speech goes something like this:

You should write something every day. That's over and above and beyond what you write in your journal every day, which by the way, is due this Friday as it is every Friday which goes without saying but I feel "behooved" to say it anyway. Let's say you are writing a note to pin on your door saying you'll be back in a minute. Put a couple of extra sentences in it. Write long notes to your brother telling what you think of him — in detail. Write a page describing the girl you like. Leave it somewhere where she'll find it. If you're shy, sign someone else's name. Doesn't matter. As long as you get the practice. Better still, keep all these things. Put them in a file system. Build up a file of daily bits of writing. Write down what you hear people say. Write letters to your friends. Don't send them. Write to the newspaper. Keep the letters. File them. Write to your dead great-grandmother. File the letter under "L" for letters. Or, better still, under "G" for great-granny.

Some geese fly over. You hear them. You see them. Write it down. Three or four sentences. What are they like? Put the geese under "G" with your great-grandmother.

They send you to the hardware store for a plug. You get the wrong plug. They send you back. You feel stupid. You *are* stupid. Write it down. How it feels to be stupid about plugs. Put it under "S." "S" for stupid.

You feed some sheep at the Experimental Farm. Everybody thinks all sheep look the same. They're wrong. Sheep look different from each other. You know that. Write it down. One sheep looks like she's just been told she owes a thousand dollars extra income tax. The next sheep looks like she's going to cry. The next one looks like he just robbed a gas station. The next one looks like she's drunk. Write it down. Put it under "S." "S" for sheep. Practise. Practise . . . "

It's a pretty good speech.

So it was because of my English teacher constantly telling us to write all the time that I wrote Sibyl Vane's absentee note for her. She tried to tell me what to write. She said to put: "Please excuse Sibyl's absence yesterday as she was sick." I didn't think that was good enough so I wrote this:

Dear Mrs. Black:

Sibyl was so sick yesterday that her head and feet swelled up so that she hardly looked human. The bandages

I wrapped around her entire body burst around suppertime
and purple pus squirted out. When the doctor finally
arrived and saw Sibyl he couldn't handle it and ran out
the door screaming, his hands covering his face . . . so how
do you expect my daughter to show up at school in that
kind of shape?
Yours truly,
Sibyl's Mom,
Mrs. S. Vane

Sibyl never bothered to open the note and read it over. Sibyl hates reading and writing but she always gets good marks in school. I don't know how she does it. The reason she asked me to write it for her was that I told her secretly that I liked to write, but not school work writing and not to tell anybody.

I confided in her because I thought if I did she'd let me kiss her, but it didn't work. I think she lets "The King" kiss her and probably do a whole lot more.

Oh, well.

Anyway, Mrs. Black took a fit and showed the letter to Mr. Black, alias the principal, and I guess he phoned Mrs. Vane and then Sibyl-the-big-suck confessed and down to the office I went. The charge — forgery!

The two Blacks got me in the office and worked me over.

~

That Mrs. Black, she can cause you to shiver just by looking at you. The kids who have her as a teacher all say that you should never look in her eyes or she'll hypnotize you. I don't think it's her eyes so much, it's her eyebrows. She has very bushy eyebrows. And they bob up and down when she talks. Nobody can understand why Mr. Black came round to marrying her. She reminds me of a guy in the movies who always plays a homicidal-maniac-Nazi-prison-guard. And her arms are very hairy. She even has thick black hair on her knuckles.

The Blacks told me that with this kind of behaviour I will never get my Entrance Certificate and go on to high school and instant success.

And forgery, of course, is a criminal offence and Mrs. Vane is seriously considering pressing charges, having me arrested and thrown into a rat-infested dungeon while I await being hanged by the neck until I am dead — God rest my soul.

And then of course Mr. Black told my English teacher, and he lied and denied he ever encouraged his students to sign other people's names to their writing and then he kept me after school and told me about the "horrible consequences" of not getting my Entrance Certificate and "as surely as night follows day" and "without a shadow of a doubt" I was heading for a life of "debauchery" and crime. He said this "without reservation."

~

I think what I'll do is quit school and move down to America. I could become a much bigger criminal in Gotham City or Chicago than I can here at Hopewell Public School. I could become a famous bank robber and get gunned down coming out of a movie theatre showing *High Sierra* starring Humphrey Bogart and Ida Lupino. Or, better still, I could become a mobster and be sentenced to the electric chair. I'd much rather get juiced in the chair than get choked by hanging.

I sometimes feel like I'm choking when I'm just sitting in my desk at school, and I have to say "without reservation" that I don't like the feeling one bit.

~

I like going to the toilet at school because you don't have to wait. There's always lots of room. Not like at home. At home there's usually a lineup at the two toilets, men's and ladies'. There are benches along the wall where you can sit and wait. If the line is really long, I bring my journal and write in it, like I'm doing now. Not everybody sits down to wait. Some people walk around a lot and squirm. They're the ones who have to go real bad. The males are worse than the females. They can't seem to hold it in as well. Mom says that's because men lack self control. And also, she says, that their bladders are often bursting with beer.

Mom's always writing to the "authorities" about how do they expect eight families to get along with only two toilets.

And about how our building is always too hot.

And about how there's people cheating on the shower schedule. There's a list on the wall by the laundry tubs of when each unit is allowed to use the shower. People are crossing other people's names out and writing in their own. You're supposed to be able to take a hot shower every eighth day. When you do get a turn there's never any hot water anyway. So I don't bother.

I usually just go down to the laundry tubs and wet my head and then wait a while and come back.

It tricks Mom.

~

Riding into Hopewell School (alias Hopeless Public) on the Uplands bus this morning, I wondered if my friends and I stink or not.

I read in one of Mom's medical books all about bed-bugs and lice. Poor people often have bedbugs and lice. Bedbugs suck your blood at night when you're asleep. So there's tiny blobs of dead blood in your bed. When blood goes bad it smells sicky sweet, like rotting corpses. Like death!

Our gang from Uplands gets on the bus first. For some reason we all sit near the back. There's usually about 20 of us, adults going to work and school kids.

Then, along the highway by the Rideau River, the bus picks up the fancy people, the rich people from man-sions. They all sit near the front. They'll stay standing even though there might be empty seats in the middle of the bus.

There's always a big gap between the gang at the back and the groups at the front.

Sometimes, on purpose, I'll sit in a seat near the

front just to see what happens. When I do that, nobody sits beside me.

I don't think I stink, but maybe I do.

~

A couple of weeks ago while I was sitting in the bus terminal I felt something against my foot under the bench.

It was a book somebody dropped. It was called *The Picture of Dorian Gray* by Oscar Wilde. I started flipping through it, trying to make some sense out of it, when I saw a name that jumped right off the page at me like a dog jumping up to lick your face.

The name was Sibyl Vane! Sibyl Vane was the main girl in the story. Her name was in the book lots of times. Then I saw a part where she was dead. She committed suicide or was murdered. I couldn't figure out which. She was a beautiful actress. She was Dorian Gray's girl-friend. And it was his fault that she was horribly dead. Or murdered by him.

In the front of the book it told what the book was about. There were words like "debauchery" and "corruption" and "sin" and "ruined women" and "labyrinths of iniquitous dens," "torture" and "opium" and "sadism" and "murder."

Poor Sibyl Vane! In a dirty book!

See, Dorian Gray was a very handsome man, a beautiful man. He gets a picture of himself painted by an artist. He puts the picture in his attic. Then he lives a corrupt, rotten life, but it never shows on his face. He stays young and beautiful. But guess what? It's the picture in the attic that gets uglier and uglier and more and more horrible.

Dorian Gray reminds me of Phil.

Phil is very handsome. But he's ugly inside. When he gets mad his face gets twisted up like Dorian's picture of himself. When he gets drunk his moustache and his nose move around while he's yelling or telling one of his stupid jokes and laughing like a hyena.

We've got no attic at the barracks so I can't prove Phil's got a picture of himself somewhere, but I bet he has. And I bet it's getting ghastlier by the minute.

Phil sells new cars. Buicks. He always drives around in a new Buick, but everybody knows it's not his. Last summer I saw a woman get into his new Buick and they drove away laughing.

I'm worried about Mom.

Maybe I'll tell her the story of Dorian Gray.

Oh yes. I looked at every page of the book and couldn't find one dirty part. I guess I don't know how to read right.

Where was all the juicy stuff, the corruption and debauchery? I sure couldn't find it.

And what were the horrible things he did to Sibyl Vane?

I wonder if Stretch "The King" King ever read *The Picture of Dorian Gray*.

Probably not. I don't think he can even read his own name. That's what everybody says about him, anyway.

~

My metalwork teacher, "Flux" Fasken, thinks he's real funny. Our project in metalwork was to make a sugar scoop out of tin. You trace a pattern on a sheet of tin, then you cut out the pattern with tin snips and fold it all carefully and solder it together. The handle gets made separately and gets soldered on. Flux Fasken took a look at my sugar scoop, started to smile, then his belly started to shake and his face got red. Then he doubled over and started choking and laughing. Then he had to hang on to the cupboard where he keeps his soldering irons to stop himself from falling over. The test for the sugar scoop was this. You fill it with water and if it doesn't leak, you pass.

He took it over to the sink and filled it with water.

It leaked in about ten places.

"Let's look at it this way," says Flux. "You could always take it home and give it to your mother. Tell her she could use it to water her plants with!"

Real funny, Flux.

~

I'll never get my Entrance Certificate if this keeps up.

~

My second-best friend, Poop Prudhomme, drew a picture of his butt and wrote Mary Jane Ballantyne's name on it and showed it to her and she screamed and told the teacher and the teacher went after Poop and accused him of being obscene and Poop told him it was just an example of modern art and now he's kicked out of Hopeless Public for two weeks.

I don't think he'll bother to go back at all. He's done with school. Maybe I am, too.

~

Our English teacher wants us to hand in our journals but I can't hand this stuff in so I'll have to write a fake one but I don't know what to say in it. I'll just make it up. How great everything is.

~

Our neighbour next door in Unit One punched his wall and his fist came right into our place. Mom has a picture of Winston Churchill hanging over the hole.

~

My friends now are Richie, Dinny, Jamie, Mickey and Lucky. Mom doesn't approve of any of them. I'm also friends with Bonnie and Connie. Mom doesn't approve of them even worse.

Everybody tries to say Connie's my girlfriend. I don't think so. The other day Connie waited outside the principal's office. When Mr. Black came out to go and get his cup of tea like he always does, Connie bent over and farted at him.

Who wants a girlfriend like that?

~

Mom thinks it would be good for me to learn how to play the clarinet. She said, "Music has charms to soothe a savage beast." I told my English teacher that my mother thought I was a savage beast and told him what she said about music. He said she had it wrong. The saying was "to soothe a savage breast," not beast.

Mom rented a clarinet and signed me up for some lessons. On the way home from my first lesson, one of the older guys on the bus grabbed my clarinet and threw it out of the window during a huge snowstorm. He said he did it because he hated music. Now I'll never become the "King of Swing" like Benny Goodman. That's what my music teacher said. I'm filing that under "S" for sarcastic.

~

Dad: In this letter I should tell you something about me. What I'm like sometimes.

Sometimes I feel dizzy and sort of sick and I start to sweat a lot. And I can't breathe. And I can't understand what people are saying to me. And I get a feeling in my stomach like I'm afraid of something but I don't know what it is I'm afraid of. I missed school for a couple of days last week because of this feeling.

"Oh, Penman," Mom said, "what am I going to do with you?"

As you can see, Mom doesn't know what to do with me. I don't blame her. I don't know what to do with me either. Would you know?

What to do with me, I mean? Just wondering.

Somebody must know.

Anyway, here's some more of my journal.

~

My best mark in Grade Eight so far is in bread board. In woodwork we made a bread board. You glue different-coloured strips of wood together and clamp them together overnight. The next day you chip off the hard drips of glue and take off the clamps. You have a square. You trace a circle on the square and cut along the line with the band saw without sawing off your thumbs. Then the sort of round plate of wood gets put on the lathe by the teacher. The lathe spins the wood around at a scary speed while you press in the chisel and watch the wood chips fly. (Don't forget your safety goggles.)

Then you sand and shellac your perfect, round bread board until smooth and shiny.

I got a D-minus. My best mark.

I took it home and we started using it. It seemed to be working pretty well. Bread was getting sliced just right.

~

Last night Phil was drunk and yelling and Mom was screaming and all of a sudden she picked up my bread board and, with both hands, brought it down hard on Phil's head.

The board fell on the floor in three pieces.

I guess I got a D-minus because of "faulty" gluing.

I was sorry about the gluing. Maybe if it was glued better it would have knocked Phil out cold and then we could have dragged him out onto the highway and wait-ed for a truck to run over him.

~

The owner of Coulter's Drugstore right next to Hopeless Public brought Richie and me to Mr. Black with
chocolate bars. He said we stole them. My punishment
was to sit at a big table in the school library all by myself
and read *David Copperfield* by Charles Dickens.

I had to do this for two days.

I couldn't understand one word of *David Copperfield*
by Charles Dickens. No, wait. I understood the first sentence. "I am born." Anybody can understand that. I
would probably write, "I was born," but so what? Who
cares what I think? Everybody knows he must be born.
How could he write this stuff if he wasn't born?

The second day I brought my book about Dorian
Gray and put it inside the Dickens book and kept on
looking for parts that told about debauchery.

The librarian caught me and squealed on me to Mr.
Black. He doubled my punishment and "confiscated" my
Dorian Gray book. Said I'd get it back when the time
arrived for me to finally leave his school, which couldn't
come too soon for him.

~

Almost every second day my friend Dinny beats up
somebody in the schoolyard at recess. Dinny always
picks the fights and he never loses. He told me he wanted to beat up every boy in Grade Eight before he was finished. He might do it.

Dinny enjoys picking the boys who are well dressed.

Nice jackets, shirts, boots. He likes getting their own blood all over their clothes.

He punches them first in the cheek. Makes the cheekbone bleed. Then he steps back and finds another place on the kid's face.

I'm glad I'm Dinny's friend and not one of the well-dressed ones on his list.

Yesterday's massacre was interrupted by Mrs. Black. She brought Dinny and some of us spectators to her husband's interrogation room.

We watched Dinny get kicked out of school for good. No Entrance Certificate for Dinny.

Mrs. Black was glaring at me during the Entrance Certificate speech. "Your element is not welcome here," she said. Her eyebrows were going all over the place. Your element.

I looked up "element" in the big dictionary in the library. The big heavy one on the stand with all the pages. I like that big book. There was a whole page practically on "element."

There were all kinds of meanings. The one I like the best is: "One of the substances, usually earth, air, fire and water, formerly regarded as constituting the whole universe."

I think I'm fire.

~

Bonnie's with some high-school kids on the corner at noon hour. One of them has a mickey of rye. Bonnie's acting stupid. Opening her mouth and showing the sandwich she's chewing. I take a whiff of the rye from the bottle. It smells like Phil.

~

Last weekend Jamie and I robbed a bakery wagon at the shelter. Pies, doughnuts, cakes, gingersnaps. We took it all to Abandoned Barracks No. 666. Jamie had the idea to put up a sign and open a store. BAKED GOODS — CHEAP.

Our first customer was a big policeman.

We went home and I introduced Mom to the policeman. He told her Jamie tried to sell him a doughnut in the police car.

~

Lucky got dared in Science class. Dared to drink some kind of stuff. He drank some of it.

The ambulance came and took Lucky away.

~

School is over.

I got my report card. It said *Passed On Condition*. They told me *On Condition* means that I barely passed, but that if I don't do better at the beginning of Grade Nine they will send me back to Grade Eight. They said Mom would get a letter telling her about the Entrance Certificate being held back *On Condition*.

Maybe I have it — maybe I haven't.

~

There's a cobweb on the ceiling that I see every night before I go to sleep. I always say that tomorrow I'm going to get the broom and take away the cobweb. I don't want spiders falling on my face when I'm asleep.

But I always forget.

And every night it's there.

And every night I say that tomorrow I'm going to get the broom and brush it away.

And every morning, I forget.

~

I've got an armload of school crap. Report card — all Fs except English and Shop. Workbooks (empty), notebooks (almost empty), the school song, a broken math set, *The Picture of Dorian Gray* by Oscar Wilde, scribblers, a sweater, my sugar scoop good for watering plants, notes passed from Connie and a Be My Valentine card with a drawing of her lips, failed test papers, lists of missed days, three-hole-paper reinforcements, 2 pencils, Geography maps, a calendar for organizing study time (blank), a school crest to remember good ol' Hopeless Public, a photo of Sibyl Vane standing beside a car with "The King" . . .

I've missed my bus.

Along comes Bonnie.

We decide to hitchhike.

Bonnie offers me a puff on her cigarette.

She gets a ride right after she puts on a whole lot of lipstick.

They don't want me in the car.

I decide to walk.

In the middle of Billings Bridge I stop and look down at the water flowing, moving, stuff floating.

The Rideau River falls into the Ottawa River. The Ottawa River runs down to Montreal and turns left into the St. Lawrence River. Then you could turn right and go down the Atlantic Ocean and turn right again and go up the Pacific Ocean to Australia or wherever you want.

~

If I have to walk all the way home I'm not carrying all this junk all that way — more than four miles.

I throw it all off Billings Bridge into the Rideau River and watch it float, slow and quiet, away.

All this school crap, floating further and further away from me.

To somewhere far away from here.

END OF SOME OF MY JOURNAL

P.P.P.S.
There.
That should do it.
signed, Penman

P.P.P.P.S.
As you can see, Dad, I'm fine.
And I'm not doing much.
signed, Penman

P.P.P.P.P.S.
Try and not forget my birthday this time.
signed, Penman

P.P.P.P.P.P.S.
Bye for now. Until you arrive.
signed, Penman

P.P.P.P.P.P.P.S.
I hope.
signed, Penman

169

*Though Solomon's family are free Blacks, a close call
with slavecatchers, from which Solomon
barely escapes, impels them to move from Virginia
to Canada West. But racism follows them even here,
and rears its head when Solomon is expelled from his local
school simply because he's not white.*

AFUA COOPER *is a scholar and poet who has studied
Black communities in Ontario during the 1800s.*

To Learn . . . Even a Little

⤬

The Letters of Solomon Washington

Village of Charlotteville, Canada West
February 1853 – August 1854

15 February 1853
To Julius Solomon
Charlottesville, Norfolk County, Virginia,
United States of America

My dear cousin Julius,

I received your letter and happily read all its contents. To think that you are to be attending a coloured college in the nation's capital. We are all so proud of you and expect you to do some great thing with your life. Receiving your letter cheered me up a great deal, and believe me, Julius, I am in need of good cheer. My news is exactly the opposite of yours. I have been expelled from my school! Expelled by the school trustee, one Mr. Philip Glasgow, who rode to the school in his wagon and right in front of my classmates told me to pack my things and leave the school immediately. Confused, I asked him why. "Why?" he shouted at me. "Because Anglo-Saxon civilization will not be trampled upon by African barbarity!"

Julius, those were his exact words. I had no idea what he was talking about, but as he stood glowering at me I picked up my satchel and left the room while some of my classmates booed and made jeering sounds. "That is what you get for fighting with your classmates," my teacher yelled as I walked from the room. It was then I knew why I was expelled. I walked the mile and a half home to our farm.

Let me explain about the fight. Yesterday I got into a fight with four of my classmates in our schoolyard. For the whole school year, I have been teased by these bullies. Making reference to my complexion, they called me the meanest names — I am sure you can imagine what they are. These boys began to pound me with their fists; another broke a limb from a nearby tree and began hitting me with it. I defended myself, of course, using the fighting techniques that my father taught me. In short order, I beat them up.

Soon after, our teacher approached the scene and began shouting at me. He said he was watching the fight from the doorway of the school and could see that I was the aggressor. The four boys agreed with him. I asked him how and why I would attack four boys. I asked him if he had heard the mean names they had called me. He said not to ask him anything and that I was rude and saucy. He then told me to "get on home" and not to come back to school without bringing my father.

As soon as I reached home, I had to tell my parents what happened — they could see I was bleeding. I explained that I could not return to school until Father accompanied me. My mother bathed my bruises and did the best she could with her potions. But I felt alone, sad and degraded. Father was angry and wanted to go out into the night to the teacher's house and demand an explanation for the cuts, the bruises and the expulsion, but Mother feared that the teacher would call the constables and get Father arrested. So we waited until the next morning.

We arrived at the school early this morning. The four boys, their fathers, and the trustee, Mr. Glasgow, were already there. Our teacher sent the rest of the scholars outside to play and called a meeting. I related my side of the story, how for months I had been the target of racial abuse. The four boys merely said that whenever I passed them I "glowered." Their fathers said they were thinking of pressing charges against me for beating up their sons. Not once did any of them acknowledge that their sons had attacked me. I think they were all embarrassed that I, one person, had laid low all four of them.

But the teacher sided fully with the boys. My father rankled with the unfairness of it all and said that he pays the school tax and therefore I have every right to be in the school and should be able to learn without fear.

This is how the meeting ended, Julius. Father left, along with the trustee and the four fathers. The teacher then told me I should sit at the back of the classroom. Shortly after, Mr. Glasgow came back and told me I was expelled. He also gave the same news to the four other Black boys in the school. Father had already left by then, so I went home and gave my parents the news. Father rode to the trustee's house to find out why. Mr. Glasgow told him that the school was only for white children, that Mr. Ryerson, who is the chief superintendent of education, had established a school for Black children in the town of Simcoe. The trustee said that was the school I should attend.

Father reminded Mr. Glasgow that he pays the school tax for the section of Norfolk County where we live and where our school is, but the trustee repeated that the Norfolk school is for white scholars and white scholars alone. He repeated that the five Black scholars who were dismissed must go to the separate school in Simcoe.

Julius, here is the most ridiculous part of it — that school sits closed and shuttered for over a year now for want of a teacher. And even if it was not closed it is eight miles away, and not even near the section where we live.

My father says he will not accept my expulsion. He has a plan, but for now he keeps it to himself.

Mother has just appeared and told me it is very late and I must turn the lamp off and get to sleep. Why should it matter? I have no school in the morrow. But I shall obey her and be off to bed. I will send you another letter soon.

From your dear cousin Solomon Washington

Dear Julius,

I find it comforting to be able to use this letter to unburden myself — though I hope it is not difficult for you to hear of our troubles. You have been like a big brother to me. I will always remember how you rescued me from kidnappers when I was only seven. I can still see that day — you and I playing in Grandfather's apple orchard when those two white men crept up behind us and began to drag us to their horses. My mouth was covered; I could not scream. But you did. Remember how our fathers and grandfather came running and fought off the kidnappers? That was what persuaded my parents to leave the United States and move to Canada. Father said that free Blacks should never have to live in fear of being abducted. I shudder to think of my fate had I been sold into slavery.

The entire household is upset because of the expulsion. My father sits and writes letters. My mother sings all the time — it seems to soothe her. The twins look at me with sad eyes. Ramona, who is more sensitive than Charles, cries whenever I emerge from my room and tells me she loves me. God bless her.

It is fortunate that you have a coloured private school for your younger brothers to attend. Now I better understand your father's feelings in wanting to go to Liberia. My father says that the disadvantages we suffer in both countries are enough to make anyone desire to leave and search for a better place.

Canada was supposed to be our better place.

And for a while it was.

When we arrived from Virginia seven years ago and settled in Sandwich so Father could begin farming, we were disappointed that there were no schools for coloured children and that they were prevented from attending the local common schools. That is why Mrs. Mary Bibb was moved to open a school for the Black children. I have probably told you that she was a wonderful teacher. She taught us how to love words. Every Friday afternoon we had elocution lessons and once a month we prepared and gave speeches on topics she chose. Young as we were, we learnt many new words and learning was a joy.

Leaving Mrs. Bibb's school was the reason I was so sad when we moved from Sandwich to Charlotteville. But since Father had purchased a bigger farm here and was intent on growing tobacco, I had no choice. He said that in Charlotteville there would be lots of opportunities.

But the opposite was true, as you know from some of my earlier letters. The people here feel that Black people are too ambitious. Some of our Black neighbours' farmhouses were even burnt — arson was the cause. It seemed that everyone knew who the arsonist was but no one would speak. And the looks we receive when we go into town, the whispers and sneers.

The teacher here in Charlotteville mocked my

speech. He said I should speak like the Negro that I was and not to speak white. It hurt me more than words could say. So I only spoke when I had to. Now that I think of it, my teacher was a bully just like my class-mates.

My parents knew of my sufferings, I am sure, but when they asked me about school I told them everything was fine. And I held back on writing to you about some of my problems too, until recently.

I am still unable to go to school. But my time is taken up with work on the farm. It is almost the end of winter and there is a lot to be done to prepare for the planting season.

I enjoy taking out the horses for exercise. Frederick is my favourite, as you know. One of the things I like best is to ride him down to Port Dover and trot along the beach there. I look over the expanse of the lake, beyond the horizon, and know that on the other side is the land of my birth and yours too, the United States. I think of you on the other side, in Virginia.

I think that my parents came to Canada West to find freedom, which in many respects has been denied. Did they make the right decision to come here?

I love Lake Erie. I love coming and sitting by the water and listening to its murmurings. It calms me and makes me think that better will come. Frederick usually comes and stands beside me, as if he understands what I am going through. I think he does. Animals sometimes are more sensitive than people.

In some of my free moments, I teach Ramona and Charles their letters and have begun teaching them to read. I also do simple sums with them. But my own learning is suffering. I have read and re-read the books we have at home. I am now in the process of reading the Bible from cover to cover and have now arrived at the end of Exodus.

At this moment in the province, a great debate rages on about whether or not Black scholars should be allowed to attend the common schools. All parents must pay the school tax, and the coloured parents pay their tax but find they are blocked in sending their children to school. The white people have said that Mr. Ryerson has established schools for the Black scholars and they must go to *those* schools. It is true that in some towns and villages there are those schools, but not in most. And yet I am expected to attend that one. When Mr. Ryerson came up with that idea it was because so many Black scholars were being turned away that their parents asked him to intervene. But he did not mean that these scholars would be barred from attending a local school if there was one in the district where they lived.

When the whites realize that their argument is wrong, they resort to other means, like declaring the common schools to be private schools, or changing the boundaries of the school districts to exclude farms owned by Black people. Father explained that this is called gerrymandering and that it is the worst way to deny our people their rights.

As for me, I feel the worst kind of betrayal. I have lived most of my life in this country; I have as much right as anyone else to education and respect. But what I feel most of all is sadness. A deep sadness that rises within me when I wake up and that goes to bed with me when I sleep.

I close with abiding respect.
Your cousin Solomon

P.S. Julius, I feel at ease in telling you about my problems. There is not another boy living close by that I could confide in. Over the years we have written to each other and you have become my best friend even though you live far away. I hope you don't find my letter too complaining. I do not want to unburden myself to my parents. They have enough problems of their own.

15 May 1853

Dear Julius,

Thank you for your letter of 30 April. So the die is cast and your entire family is moving to Liberia! I regret to hear that that Black children in Virginia face the same problem as our situation with the common school here, and so your father has come to the conclusion that Blacks would not find freedom anywhere in North America and he has decided to remove your family to Liberia.

After your mention of that country in an earlier letter, I have been reading about the Liberian migrations in *The Voice of the Fugitive,* our own newspaper here in the province. It is published by Mr. Henry Bibb, husband of my teacher Mrs. Mary Bibb, and himself a fugitive from American slavery. Many are opposed to the movement to Liberia, while others think it is the only hope for our race. They think it makes sense to go to a place where we are wanted and where we can contribute with our skills and talents.

I must confess though that I do not want you to go. You are our only family on this continent. How I would miss you! But my reasons are selfish. I wish only for your good and that of your family. But what will happen to your college studies? The last we heard, you were planning to attend the Colored College of Washington D.C. in August.

There is some good news on my front. My mother found a school for me. Here is what happened. Mother and the parents of the other scholars who were expelled from our school approached our pastor, the Reverend Sorrick, to tutor us. He's the Reverend of the local British Methodist Episcopal church. After considering the request, Reverend Sorrick converted his parlour into a classroom, and every Tuesday and Thursday evening I ride to our new school. My parents pay him a fee for his efforts. This gives me a welcome chance for an outing on Frederick too.

I study Penmanship, Mathematics, Grammar, Bible Studies, Reading and Ancient History. Reverend Sorrick also introduced us to a subject called Rhetoric, and rudimentary Greek and Latin. The Reverend has the largest collection of books I have ever seen. At my former school our teacher had a few books which he kept locked in a cabinet. There is a library of sorts in Simcoe, but you have to pay to use it and it is only opened to the whites.

The Reverend has books on every topic under the sun. One afternoon I arrived early before our class started and I took the time to look through some of the shelves. The Reverend tells me he orders his books from booksellers in Montreal and Boston. Needless to say, I am more than impressed with his library. I wish one day to have as many books as he does. (My father says that the Reverend is not only one of the most accomplished Black men in Canada, but one of the most educated persons in the entire country.) I do not know how long our little academy will last, because I was told that the Reverend is thinking of taking up a post in Bermuda where the BME church has also established itself.

Reverend Sorrick attended Oberlin College. I dream of going there one day. As you may know, it is the only school in America that accepts white and Black scholars, both male and female.

We greatly admire Reverend Sorrick. He is so well-spoken, and has a deep and sonorous voice. I see in him what I can become later in life. (He expresses a wish that it would be good for me to go into the ministry. My father however wants me to become a doctor.)

I must go now to make some bee boxes; Mother is determined to become a beekeeper. I will write again tomorrow.

16 May 1853

Dear Julius,

Mother called to me to put out my light last night before my letter was finished, so I'll continue now.

Studying with the Reverend has brought me a new joy. I am much happier than I was. I love to discover new things, new ideas, new words, and new ways of thinking. I love reading stories like Homer's *Odyssey* (in translation of course). I would be the happiest person alive if I could spend my time studying and learning. Maybe the Reverend knows me more than I know myself. I now see that Oberlin College could be a possibility. I seem to have a new energy.

There is one more thing I want to put in this letter before I send it. The school trustees of Charlotteville are determined that I not set foot in the common school again. They have changed the boundaries of the school district by running a line through it that excludes our house from that particular district. They then sent a letter to my father saying that our 80 acres is excluded from the limits. Father says he is one of the largest taxpayers in this county, and has given 12 free days of labour to the county (6 more days than the required number) and that he is entitled to his rights.

I must say my goodbye to you. It is late and I hear Mother's footsteps. I know she is coming to tell me to turn off the lamplight again. God's blessings on you and your family.

Your cousin and humble servant,
Solomon

30 May 1853

Dear Julius,

Ramona and Charles are becoming excellent readers. Both read with ease the *Irish Reader, Book One* and are now tackling *Book Two*. I have also taught them to cipher. Father and I have commenced planting the new tobacco, and next week we will be raising a new barn with the help of our friends and neighbours.

There is even better news! And that is why I write to you even before I get a response from you to my previous letter. My father did it — he sued the school trustees. In fact, he sued the entire school board. And the matter is to be heard in court soon. Remember I told you that he was always writing letters? Well, he was writing to Mr. Egerton Ryerson, the superintendent for education for all of Canada West. He told Mr. Ryerson what had happened to me and asked for advice on how to proceed. The advice the superintendent gave Father was for him to sue the trustees!

The lawyer that Father retained is Mr. George

Hanson, who recently opened a practice in Simcoe. He has charged the trustees with wrongful dismissal, racial prejudice, gerrymandering the boundaries of the school district, and denial of education for me.

The whole thing has caused a stir. Whenever my father and I go into town to buy supplies or sell our produce, people stop as we approach in our wagon, point at us and murmur among themselves. Sometimes, they become abusive. When Father and I went to Mr. Copperfield, the town's agent for tobacco, he refused to buy our cured tobacco from last year, saying that we had grown too big for our breeches, and that we should be grateful to be living in Canada, and ought to behave ourselves instead of making trouble and suing the school board. My father bore the abuse silently, and the following day took the tobacco to Hamilton to sell it to an agent there.

Black folks from all over the district have been coming to our farm to speak to my parents. Some of them have also had their children chased from the common school. The parents see my father as a kind of hero for challenging the school board. Sometimes they bring gifts of food and produce to us. A few give money to help with the court case. Everywhere the same story is repeated — Black children turned out of school and denied an education — in Amherstburg, Windsor, Hamilton, Brantford, Ancaster. All over the province.

The Reverend Sorrick has become a regular visitor to our house. He comes to pray with us and offer spiritual guidance. As we wait for the court date I am excited, but fearful at the same time. What will the outcome be?

I will write soon. Please send me your news, especially about the move to Liberia, and give my best regards to your family.

Your cousin,
Solomon Washington

18 July 1853

Dear Julius,

We went to court this morning. We lost. The judge said that the trustees are fully within their rights to allow who they want to in the schools, and that the African pupils must attend the coloured school. When our lawyer Mr. Hanson told the judge that the coloured school has been closed for over a year for want of a teacher and also because not enough children live in that section, the judge said he did not care. He said he is following the books, and that the Provincial School Act states that wherever there was a coloured school, it is that school the coloured children must attend.

There was booing in the court after he rendered judgement. It was the Black citizens, of course. I was never more dejected in my life after hearing such a decision. Immediately Mr. Hanson walked over to my father and said he would appeal the decision to the Court of King's Bench in Toronto. He said we will never get justice here because one of the school trustees is related to the judge.

I will let you know how this is all progressing (or not). I am waiting to hear more of your plans to move.

Your cousin,
Solomon

17 August 1854

Dear Julius,

It is nearly a year since my last letter to you. The last one I received from you was dated 8 November 1853. We rejoiced that you all had arrived in Liberia safely, found a place to live, and that you are in college and your two brothers in an academy. Liberia and its capital Monrovia sound too good to be true. I read your letter over and over. I did reply and, not hearing from you for months, I assumed you did not receive my letter.

We were all worried, not hearing from you or your family. I wrote you several letters after that but did not hear a word back. So imagine my great surprise and joy when I received a letter from you in May asking me why I had not written! My letters must have been lost at sea, or perhaps were not sent on to you after your family left for Liberia. Your letter arrived at the right moment, because a great event recently took place in my life. I will tell you of it shortly. I am hoping you will get this letter.

There is so much news to report. I am now nearly a

year older, of course, and have grown to over five feet and nine inches. People think I am older than my fifteen years. I continued with Reverend Sorrick until January of this year, when he closed the academy for two main reasons. We had a very cold winter with lots of snow; this made travelling difficult at times. He was also preparing to move to Bermuda. Secondly, my labour was needed at home full time — one reason being my mother was expecting a new baby and had not been well. I must report, dear Julius, that you are now the proud cousin of a new baby girl. Mother has named her Patience Liberty. I leave you to work out the meaning of her name.

The twins have gotten big. They are now excellent readers for children of seven years old and are progressing through *Book Three* of the Irish series. I believe they are little prodigies but I am partial toward them, being their older brother and teacher.

You must be wondering about the outcome of the lawsuit against the trustees. I will no longer hold you in suspense. Mr. Hanson appealed the case to the highest court in the land, the Court of King's Bench. Mr. Hanson believed that was the only place where we had a chance of getting some justice.

My father and I travelled to Toronto for the trial, which was held on 17 June. What a marvellous place it is. The buildings are splendid and tall. Never in my life have I seen so many carriages and wagons moving along the streets. If you are not careful you will be run over by these vehicles. (There is a cab company there that was founded by a Black man named Thornton Blackburn. He is a refugee from Kentucky slavery. He has become a wealthy man from his cab business.) In Toronto, the people all wear fine clothing. We stayed at a lodging house run by two of my father's friends from Virginia.

Our case was called up at the Court of King's Bench, and the highest judge in the land — the chief justice, John Beverley Robinson — presided. My father told me that Mr. Robinson's father was a Virginian Loyalist and slaveowner. I did not have much trust in this Judge Robinson. It is known that last year he ruled against a Black man named Dennis Hill. Mr. Hill, like my father, had sued the trustees of his town for refusing his son entry to the local school. When it went to court, Judge Robinson said that the trustees were fully within the law to exclude Mr. Hill's son. I wondered if we could expect justice from such a judge.

While we waited inside for the judge to arrive, a tall and striking-looking Black man approached our group. Mr. Hanson quickly grabbed his hand and gave him a powerful handshake. He introduced the man to us, a Mr. Robert Sutherland, a lawyer! Mr. Sutherland is the first Black lawyer to be trained in Canada. He is from the island of Jamaica and attended Queen's College in this province. He and Mr. Hanson were classmates at Queen's, and Mr. Hanson said Mr. Sutherland won four-teen academic prizes, including Latin and Mathematics, during their graduating year. Mr. Sutherland talked with Mr. Hanson and my father about what sounded like some obscure points of our case. Mr. Hanson nodded his head throughout the conversation. During the whole time, I was in awe of Mr. Sutherland. A coloured lawyer and one who knows the law like the back of his hand!

The judged arrived looking very much the aristocrat he was rumoured to be. I could not forget his slave-holding background. I hoped he had a bone of fairness in him. The lawyer for the trustees presented their case, while Philip Glasgow — you will remember that he is the head trustee, the one who expelled me — stood glowering at me and my father. Mr. Hanson presented our case. The judge listened and took notes. Then he called a recess. I did not have much hope, but Mr. Hanson seemed to think that we would get some justice.

After what seemed like a long time, Mr. Robinson returned and gave his decision. He ruled in our favour! Here is what he said: "There are no separate schools for Blacks in Charlotteville. The effects of attempts to run a school-district line that would exclude the plaintiff's (my father's) land were to deprive him of schooling entirely. Simply because there was no other school, the plaintiff must be given access to the common schools."

After a year of fighting the school trustees of Charlotteville, Julius, we finally gained justice. Mr. Glasgow stormed out of the court upon hearing Judge Robinson's verdict. Mr. Hanson came and shook my hands vigorously. I was beyond myself with joy, and hugged my father.

We returned home two days later. We took the stage

to Hamilton and from there another stage to Simcoe. Mr. Sidney Crosby was waiting for us in his wagon. News of our victory had travelled ahead of us. Mr. Crosby threw his hat up in the air when he saw us.

As we journeyed through the countryside, I reflected on my family's journey in fighting for me to get an education. All they want is for me to learn . . . even a little. I will never forget that my father would not give up. Nor will I forget my mother's persistence that I not fall behind. I will also remember the meanness of the teacher and the school trustees for denying education to children. Prejudice against colour is an evil thing.

You might remember me saying that Reverend Sorrick and my mother want me to become a minister; my father, a doctor. But after seeing Mr. Hanson in court, and experiencing how the law can be used to get justice, an idea has begun forming in my mind that that is the path I would like to pursue. To become a lawyer and help those who are in need of such help. It is not a far-fetched idea for a Black boy to become a lawyer. Just look at Mr. Sutherland!

But though Judge Robinson ruled I could return to the common school, do I really want to go back to a place where the teacher, scholars and trustees seek ways to destroy me?

As if reading my thoughts, Mr. Crosby turned around, a huge smile on his face. "You wouldn't believe what happened," he said. Father and I looked at him curiously. "Well, with all the excitement about the court case, the school teacher and trustee Glasgow are leaving the area. It is rumoured that they are going out west to homestead in a place called the Red River District. They say in the Red River a man can get hundreds of acres for free." He also added that the school might get a new teacher.

I am sitting on the back porch writing you this letter, Julius. I feel like my whole future is a big question mark, but I must think that better times are ahead with the court case behind us and a new teacher coming to school. I have fallen behind for a year, but with hard work, I will catch up. My one regret is that Father had to sell Frederick to help pay our legal costs. That was so hard, but at least our case prevailed, and Father says he will do what he can to get Frederick back.

The sun is setting and the light is fading. A company of people have arrived for a dinner arranged by my mother, ready to celebrate our victory. The first wagon has just rolled into the yard, so I must close this letter soon. Who knows? Maybe one day I will become a lawyer and move to Liberia to help my countrymen there.

I must go. Dear Julius, I pray that you will receive this letter. My kindest regards to you, my uncle, my aunt and your two brothers. My dear cousin, pray for me and my family, as I pray for you and yours. God bless you and Liberia too.

Your cousin and humble servant,
Solomon Washington

*Living through the Depression is hard enough to cope with,
and then there's the fire that took away everything that
Yvonne's family held dear . . . She hopes that the move
to Thetford Mines will mark a new beginning.
But there are other hurdles to overcome.*

*Several of the events included in Yvonne's diary spring from
actual stories that* **MARIE-ANDRÉE CLERMONT** *heard
during the summers she spent in her grandparents' home
in Thetford Mines during her childhood
and teenage years.*

Out of the Ashes

☙

The Diary of Yvonne Boissonneault

Thetford Mines, Québec
November – December 1938

Sunday, November 27 (late)

I did something awful, Journal. Maman and Papa were having another fight and I listened in. I wasn't really eavesdropping. I was writing in you, sitting in my closet, and first thing I knew, they were in their room yelling at each other. With the walls so thin, I could hear everything.

Living at Grand-Papa's isn't easy for any of us, but it's even harder for Maman. She shouted at Papa about his father being a tyrant and ordering her around as if she were his servant. And about Thetford Mines being so polluted. Angrier by the minute, she spilled an endless list of complaints. "You think I enjoy cleaning the house morning and night so we don't breathe asbestos dust?" she said with such fury that my heart stopped beating. A scream was wailing silently at the back of my throat.

Then Papa spoke back, about how could Maman be so ungrateful, and that without his father's help, we would have no home and Papa would be out of a job.

"We lost *everything* in that fire, remember?" he said. "Would you rather be starving in Abitibi?"

We all know that the workshop provided our income back in Abitibi, and that asbestos is the reason this region might overcome the hardships of the Depression faster than others. And I didn't need to be reminded that Thetford is a dusty town.

They started nagging at each other so I blocked my ears. When I listened again after a long while, they were talking more quietly. Papa was urging Maman to make the most of the situation, reminding her how strong she is. But she didn't let him finish. "My strength went up in smoke when our house burned down," she said. Then she grumbled about this house not feeling like home when she can't even move one piece of furniture without Grand-Papa going berserk.

Then their voices lowered and I had to strain to hear Papa say, "Come, into my arms, Rachel. Let's kiss and make up." But Maman started sobbing, and it went on and on and on, so I crawled out of the closet and here I am, writing in the bathroom. It's almost midnight and I feel terrible.

Monday, November 28

Drat! DRAT! <u>DRAT!</u> for all that went wrong today. Journal, I was spanked this morning, by my mother, who claims she doesn't believe in corporal punishment. HUMILIATION!

Also, I'm in BIG trouble at school.

Maman burst into our room really early, demanding our help because there was just too much work for her to do alone. She was nervous and she looked terrible. She probably hadn't slept all night. She told Laura that every morning before breakfast she was to sweep the upstairs floors. Saint Laura nodded. Then Maman said that I would make all the beds and pick up whatever is on the floor. Seeing me scowl, she added that she would clean downstairs, so I don't have to do Grand-Papa's room.

I made a face. What about Bernard? He's seventeen, after all. Can't he make his own bed? Why do Laura and I have to do it all?

Bernard's responsibilities are to keep the woodbox supplied for the stove, Maman retorted, and to run errands for Papa at the store. Even as Maman was listing our chores, my brother wandered out of the bathroom and walked past our room, sticking his tongue out at me. "Yvonne-la-grognonne," I heard him singsong on his way downstairs. The brat, calling me grumpy! I was seething. Maman said she understood how hard it was coping with the loss of our home and then moving here to a new town, but that we must adjust.

There are always tears in her voice when she recalls our former life. Not only did she lose everything she owned in that fire, but it's as though a giant eraser wiped away all the years she'd spent building our family life, all those special routines that knit us together and made us feel so cosy. She hasn't been the same since, and I'm wondering if we'll ever regain the happiness we had before.

Journal, Laura really is a saint. She dressed quickly and started sweeping. But I yawned, went to the bathroom, took my time putting on my school uniform, and then slowly started making beds. Mine. Laura's. I worked faster in my parents' bedroom to escape the angry emotions floating about. The little ones were babbling when I came into their room, so I played with them for a bit. Then Martine helped me tidy the sheets and Charles threw his playthings in the toy box for me.

I had no intention of making Bernard's bed. The simple thought repulsed me. And the view of his pyjamas lying in a heap made my insides turn over, not to mention his crumpled sheets. To cap it all off, his pillow was nagging at me from the top of the huge armoire — out of reach.

"I will *not* do this!" I muttered.

Maman must have heard me, for she came right up and glared at me. But I stamped my foot, hollering that my "pig brother" could pick up his own rubbish, and that I would *not* clean that dump!

That's when Maman grabbed me, pulled me into my room and spanked me. Hard. After that, she forced me to make Bernard's bed. Then she marched me down the stairs, bundled me into my coat and sent me off to school. She gave me a piece of bread to eat on the way, pushed me out with my school bag and shut the door. I stood on the steps, unable to move.

I couldn't believe this was happening, Journal. I wanted to cry. I was hurting. I felt miserable and angry.

Did Maman still love me? Why was she cruel like that? Does she forget that I lost *my* home in the fire too?

Then I turned around and saw her in the window, watching me. Her face seemed so sad that I was overcome by a terrible feeling of guilt, and I blamed myself all the way to school for making her even more unhappy.

Journal, when it rains, it pours. In school, today . . .

Oops, later. Maman's calling . . . Dusting duty . . . DRAT!

After supper

It was still very tense at the table tonight, although Maman cooked my favourite supper: shepherd's pie and maple pudding. We washed dishes really fast and then the others gathered around the piano to sing carols. Laura is a good pianist, and the little ones always love those carols. So, let them have their musical moment. I have things to write, and Bernard is splitting wood again, so I'm safe from his cheekiness.

In class, I got back my composition assignment with a ZERO scribbled across it. I was stunned. Mère Saint-Armand had asked us to recall an important event in our lives, and I had tried to write an interesting story. Back in Abitibi, Composition was my best subject and I always got good marks.

"What a beautiful text!" Mère Saint-Armand exclaimed sarcastically. She went on about my nice long sentences, well-chosen verbs, great sense of rhythm. That's when she shocked me by saying, "The problem is, you obviously copied the whole thing. I'll have you know, Mademoiselle Boissonneault, that I will not tolerate cheating."

She had called me to her desk and was scolding me in front of my classmates. My heart sank and I hung my head as she went on describing the evilness of plagiarism.

"But, Mère Saint-Armand, I did *not* copy, I swear!" I told her.

She just sneered and said that lying on top of cheating wouldn't help, "and swearing even less," but that since I like copying so much, I would no doubt enjoy transcribing one full page of the gospel as punishment. "Bring it to me tomorrow morning," she snapped. "And you will have both your parents sign your assignment, so they know what a cheat they have for a daughter."

With that, she sent me to my place and started teaching a lesson I didn't hear a word of. All I could think was, *I did not cheat, I did not cheat, I did not cheat. And I'll prove it.*

But how? With Maman in the mood she's in, I'll be in even more trouble if she thinks I cheated. I know I have to show her my

Later on

I had to run downstairs to answer the doorbell.

Thank God for Oncle Albert! He's so nice and friendly! He stopped by with my cousin Colette to say hello. I wish Colette and I were in the same Grade Six class because we're such good friends, but she goes to English school because Aunt Harriet is Irish. We gathered in the living room and, while Oncle Albert was telling funny anecdotes — even Maman laughed — I took Colette upstairs and told her about my essay problem. "Trust your parents," she advised, adding that they'd know I wrote it myself and would tell my teacher.

"But won't Mère Saint-Armand hate me even more if she's proven wrong?" I asked.

Colette argued that it would be much worse that my classmates think of me as a cheat. Then she asked what the composition was about.

"About the fire," I told her, and tears filled my eyes. Colette knows all about that, and what it meant for my family, of course. She took my hand and let the moment pass.

When we came back downstairs, Oncle Albert had terrific news to announce. He and a couple of his fellow workers in the mine are in the process of buying a piece of land on a nearby lake. If all goes according to plan, he'll take us swimming there next summer. Won't that be wonderful? Oncle Albert is Maman's "favourite brother," as she likes to say — her usual joke, because he's her only brother. Living close to him was one of the few things Maman was looking forward to when we moved here.

Their visit improved the atmosphere by one hundred per cent. After they left, I showed Maman and Papa my assignment. They believed that I wrote the essay myself — what a relief! Maman read it and said I had captured the night of the fire with a lot of insight. She wrote a note for Mère Saint-Armand, which both she and Papa signed. And of course, I was spared copying out a page of the gospel! Whew!

Monday, December 5

I've neglected you, Journal. Sorry. But I'm happy to tell you that things have improved a lot on the school front. I truly love Saint-Alphonse Convent and its formal discipline and everything, so different from my small country school in Abitibi. The convent here is an impressive four-storey building where there are rules to follow, rituals to observe, and a reputation for good teaching. The graduates have no problems finding jobs if they want to work. Some girls hear the call and eventually become nuns. Mind you, Journal, I wouldn't want that to happen to me, even if I love God and try to observe his commands. We say grace before meals at home and we attend Mass on Sundays, and I pray morning and night, but . . . it's so hard being good *all* the time. I hate Bernard, and that's a sin, and I'm lazy and selfish, and a real glutton. Besides, with that temper of mine . . . No, really, I don't have much chance of getting the call. Whew!

Anyway, Mère Saint-Armand admitted that she had misjudged me, and she apologized in class. What she said was quite nice, actually. She explained that she had sort of paid me a compliment by assuming I had cheated, because in her opinion, my text was too well written to be my own.

In class the other day, she asked us to write about someone we admired. I described Oncle Albert and got a good mark.

On the home front, Maman is still a nervous wreck. Yesterday, Papa asked her to fill in for an employee at the store who was sick, and Grand-Papa was shocked! He pointed out that a mother's place is in the home. Papa argued that he needed help to serve the customers since he — Grand-Papa — had decided to hang up his apron. In the end, Maman did go to work at the store and — I can't figure out why — it improved her mood a bit, even if it meant less time to do the chores at home.

Papa wants to start selling other foods at the store, but Grand-Papa says *Impossible!* His store is a meat shop, not a grocery store, and that's that. But according to Papa, since many people still suffer from the Depression and don't have much money to spend on food, we would attract more customers by selling rice and flour and other foods that cost less than meat. But Grand-Papa is stubborn. There is an ongoing argument about that in the house.

I make beds every morning — the usual drudgery. Bernard-the-Pest is as obnoxious as ever and I'd gladly wring his neck. He teases me every time he notices me reading, or writing in you, Journal, implying that I ought to be doing useful things instead. That's why I hide in my closet, where he can't see me. It's almost empty, anyway:

none of us has all that many clothes since the fire. Of course, his wood chopping sets Bernard free of all other house duties. It's unfair because, in reality, he loves splitting those logs. And he still has time to play bowling at the parish centre after school. He has lots of friends already. But Laura and I must come home straightaway to help, so neither of us has made any friends here yet.

I worry a lot about Maman. She is a good-looking woman, but when she's sad, her beauty is buried under her unhappiness. She used to be the prettiest mother in the world. How I miss *that* mother!

Oncle Albert is working evening shifts since last week, so he's been dropping in during the day. He raises Maman's spirits with his cheerfulness, makes the little ones laugh by fooling around, and he challenges Grand-Papa to a game of checkers. Everybody's happier when he stops by, and I can feel the lightness in the air when I come home from school.

Apart from these visits, Grand-Papa sits in his rocking chair, reading the paper or dozing off — his habit ever since he stopped working at the store and Papa took over. I think he still misses Grand-Maman — after all, it is only a year since she passed away.

Grand-Papa criticizes a lot, but one thing he's nice about is Maman's cooking. He compliments her, saying it reminds him of my grandmother's meals. I guess he didn't eat too well during the months he lived by himself. He must have felt lonely with his children scattered all over. Oncle Henri lives the closest. He has promised to treat us to a sugaring-off party next spring at his maple grove in Beauce. Oncle Henri will be here on New Year's Day — with his wife and all eight children — to receive Grand-Papa's solemn Blessing with all of us.

Journal, I'm going in every direction tonight, aren't I? What can I say? No news is good news.

Thursday, December 8

Journal, it's just horrifying! I was awakened by hushed voices and tearful moans in the middle of the night. I figured Maman and Papa were fighting again, so I blocked my ears and buried my head in my pillow. But it wasn't that at all. And the second Laura and I came downstairs this morning, I knew something much worse had happened. Maman looked dazed. Her face was all swollen and red. Papa, who's normally gone to work at this hour, was still here. And Grand-Papa, who usually sleeps much later, was up. Both seemed in shock. My heart missed a beat.

Grand-Papa was eventually able to tell the terrible news. "Your uncle died." His voice was hoarse. "A terrible accident happened at the mine last night . . . a wall fell over some miners who were cleaning debris in the entrance of a tunnel where there had been a blasting operation . . ."

"Not Oncle Albert!" I screamed and threw myself into Maman's arms.

I'm still crying as I'm writing, Journal. I'm devastated. It's so unfair. SEVEN MINERS DIED. SEVEN!

We're going to see Aunt Harriet and Colette later. Maman will cook tons of food to bring them. Laura and I will make heaps of sandwiches. No school for us today. Poor Colette! Losing a parent must be heartbreaking, and much more so in an accident like that!

Sunday, December 11

The funeral yesterday was the saddest moment of my life. Saint-Alphonse Church was full, and hundreds more people were massed outside, even in the rotten weather we had. I never thought adults could cry so hard. Seeing the seven coffins aligned side by side . . . it's indescribable. People were sobbing. Even Martine and Charles started crying nervously when Maman burst into tears during the ceremony. Laura and I had to sit them on our laps and rock them gently until they stopped. But as soon as they were soothed, they started racing up and down the aisle and we had to run after them to calm them down. Poor little kids! They are too young to figure out what's happening.

As I was sitting there in church, though, it wasn't only sadness that I felt. Yes, we lost our house to fire last summer, but we all escaped safely and were given a chance to rebuild our lives. But my uncle died in this accident. Death is so definite.

Colette is alone with Aunt Harriet now. How will they cope? They were really brave during the last few days, receiving condolences from all the relatives and friends. But now they're back in their empty house, without him. It will be a depressing Christmas for them.

I spent hours with Colette without ever being able to find words to comfort her. I was so sad myself. We just cried together. Once she talked about the land Oncle Albert wanted to buy on that lake — now a shattered dream. Another time, she started to reminisce. How great a father he was, how thoughtful and kind, how he liked to sing and clown around . . . I just listened. Later, she thanked me for being with her when she needed to talk.

I'm not crying anymore, Journal. Sad as I am that Oncle Albert's gone, I'm filled with a frantic sense of joy that Maman, Papa and the rest of us didn't die in the fire. All of us are still alive. What a strange feeling of relief! We're not as happy as before, but we're all together. I wouldn't want to lose any of them, not even Bernard. Maybe I don't really hate him, after all.

I thought Maman would be depressed when we returned home after the funeral, but she must have been reasoning just like me, because she gathered us around her for a prayer of thanks. She and Papa said beautiful words of praise to God, and we answered Amen.

Maman said she will not complain anymore. From now on, she'll make the most with what comes our way. "This house will become a happy home," she declared, and all of a sudden she seemed as pretty as I remembered her from before.

Thursday, December 15

Journal, I'm writing by Maman's bed. She's been sick with the flu for the last two days — fever, bad cough and sore throat. Laura and I miss school to take care of her, feed the family and keep the house clean. Bernard and Grand-Papa even did the laundry, and the little ones had a great time playing hide-and-seek among the clothes hanging haphazardly around the house. Everything is in upheaval.

Before Maman caught this flu, things were really getting better. She and Papa had stopped fighting, and Grand-Papa was even reconsidering Papa's idea of selling other types of food at the store.

But Maman started feeling feverish Tuesday, and had to lie down. She hasn't been out of bed since. We feed her light broth and give her the medicine Dr. Gosselin prescribed. And we keep her company when we have a chance.

Thank goodness Dr. Gosselin lives only three houses away, and that he's an old friend of Papa's. He comes to see Maman every day. Last night I heard him say that she was overworked and anaemic. He was sitting at the kitchen table with Papa, and both of them seemed so gloomy that I had goosebumps all over. Could Maman be that sick? "Her body is begging for rest," Dr. Gosselin explained. "That would account for the high fever."

And since the fever did not come down by this morning, Dr. Gosselin is making arrangements to have

Maman admitted to the hospital. I feel so bad I lost all my appetite.

Journal, I heard Maman say she might die. She was moaning, her eyes closed, her forehead burning, half asleep and a bit delirious. Still . . . hearing her say that gave me chills. Could that really happen? I've been praying non-stop ever since. *Please God, save Maman. Don't call her to you. We need her. Please God.* I even knelt and said a rosary.

I saw Bernard wipe a tear when he was chopping wood today. He's been moody ever since Oncle Albert died, and even more so since Maman took to her bed. He doesn't tease me anymore. Not that I miss it, but it makes me feel that something is very wrong. Laura tries to seem cheerful with the little ones, but it's false. When Martine and Charles are not with her, she's upset.

Must stop. Maman wants water . . .

Saturday, December 17

Maman has been in the hospital since yesterday morning and things don't look too good. Bernard, Laura and I are sitting in the living room with Grand-Papa, waiting anxiously for the doctor and Papa to come back from the hospital with some news. The little ones are asleep, but the rest of us can't even think of going to bed tonight. It's 10 p.m. and my insides are so tight I have a hard time breathing.

Later on

Maman's flu has turned into pneumonia, Journal. She's really fighting for her life tonight. A girl in my class lost her mother to that monster disease just last month. My tummy hurts and I feel light-headed. Maman can't die, can she? Dr. Gosselin is trying to make things look good, but he's really worried, I can tell. "We are trying a new medication on her," he explained. "It has given good results in the past in similar cases. So, there's hope yet." Then he took Papa aside and started whispering, but so loud that we could hear everything. He was pointing out that Oncle Albert's death, in addition to all Maman went through since the fire, had drained her endurance.

The doctor's next words were terrifying. "I'm not sure she has the strength to hold tight and fight this infection. She's worn out, Raymond. I'm sorry, but I can't be more optimistic . . . You'll have to pray for a miracle."

Papa accompanied Dr. Gosselin to the door, but we remained seated, unable to move. Grand-Papa retired to his room a few minutes ago. Papa is keeping away from us, hiding his tears. It's past midnight, Journal, and I'm not even sleepy. When he left, the doctor told Papa that he was driving back to the hospital, and I won't be able to close my eyes until we get further news. Writing helps me pass the time, but my stomach is so tight I'm afraid I'll be sick.

December 18
Early in the morning

It was about one o'clock when Bernard stood up all of a sudden, took my arm and Laura's and drew us upstairs into his room. He had an intense look on his face. He had been crying, as we all had. He closed the door. "We must do something," he whispered urgently. "But what?" asked Laura, fighting tears. Bernard was silent for a long, long time. Then he said, "Let's pray God for a miracle, like the doctor suggested."

Kneeling down, we said the Lord's Prayer and a decade of the rosary, then prayed silently. I closed my eyes, begging God to save Maman. I was terrified that she could indeed be dying.

After some time, Bernard stood up and started to talk, but ever so slowly. He was struggling to find words. His voice failed him often. "Dear God, there's . . . something I must tell you, with my sisters here as witnesses." He cleared his throat. "You have . . . been calling me, God, and I have denied your calling, burying it under a million distractions. I knew deep down that I must eventually address it, but I thought that it could wait. Well, with what's happened recently — our uncle dying and Maman being so sick — I will delay no longer."

Bernard was silent for a moment, sweat oozing from his forehead. He seemed overcome by a powerful emotion. He eventually collected himself and continued: "My answer is YES, God. If you want me, I will . . . seriously . . . consider becoming a priest."

I pinched myself hard, Journal, but I wasn't dreaming. Bernard was really making that pledge, in a solemn tone that bewildered me. I was covered with gooseflesh.

"I beg you, God, heal our mother," he added in a hoarse voice.

Laura got up and went to him. He took her in his arms. He was trembling.

And then my sister spoke. She said she was willing to give her life to save Maman's. "If you must take a life, God, take mine. As the soul of the family, Maman is needed more than I am . . . " Her voice faded away.

I gasped. Laura just couldn't die. Not at fifteen. It was unthinkable. I didn't want to lose my sister.

I was stunned by the two of them . . . I wasn't ready to offer such a giant sacrifice myself. I lacked their courage. Still, it seemed it was my turn to talk, although I had no idea of what I would say, so I slowly got to my feet, in a silence that was filled with an overpowering sense of exaltation.

Words did come to my mind, but couldn't pass my lips. I soundlessly vowed to become a better person — but that seemed so vague — and to fight against my laziness. I silently promised God to seriously work on my angry mood, to tone down my tantrums. But when I opened my mouth, I couldn't get the words out.

"I know what you could promise, Yvonne," Bernard said in an indefinable tone, and I shot him a suspicious look. He seemed sheepish all of a sudden.

"But first . . . I have a confession to make." He told

me that a few weeks ago he had stolen you, Journal, and read some entries. "And I must admit that you write beautifully," he added. "Would you believe that I was moved at times?"

I felt so angry at Bernard for violating my most intimate secrets. I fought the urge to jump in his face and shout, "You had no right!" But looking at him, I saw shame and remorse, so I burst into tears. Too much was happening at the same time. Bernard said he realized he should never have done that, and asked for my forgiveness. So what could I do? I nodded silently, but I was shaking all over.

"If you want to promise something, why don't you pledge to write the story of our family from the very beginning, especially what's happened in the last few months?" Bernard suggested. "You could get a beautiful notebook to write in. This way, none of us could ever forget. With that writing talent of yours, it certainly would be an asset to the family archives." His voice stopped, and then he managed to add, "Whatever the outcome of tonight . . . " Dread had overcome him again. I stared at him, unsure that he wasn't teasing. He wasn't.

So I nodded again and, wiping away my tears, I gratefully said the promise, with as much solemnity as I could convey.

And then the doorbell rang and we rushed downstairs with pounding hearts.

December 18, noon

I just got up, Journal. Lazy me. But it was six o'clock in the morning when I finally fell asleep. So let me tell you what happened.

When Dr. Gosselin came in, he was covered in snow, looking like a polar bear. I was watching him closely, dreading the worst. I saw a very tired man. But I thought I noticed the slightest hint of a smile hiding behind his moustache. "Your mother is getting better," he announced. "She's still very weak, but the fever's down and she's breathing normally. In other words, she is going to be all right. It will take a while, mind you, but she's on her way to recovery."

Bernard and I both had the same reflex and turned toward Laura. He moved forward just in time to catch her in his arms.

She had fainted.

Tuesday, December 20

Journal, this has been one chaotic week, what with Maman still in the hospital, and Laura being under the impression that God will come and get her any minute. The house is in turmoil, and Christmas is coming with nothing being ready. Maman is coming home in three days and we want to make everything nice for her. We're lucky that Aunt Harriet comes to help every day. She's an angel.

When Laura fainted, Bernard told Papa about Laura's pledge to God. The doctor was still here, so he just took off his coat with a deep sigh and stayed by. Then Laura regained consciousness, convinced that she was about to die. Patiently, Bernard reminded her that she had not actually *promised* to give her life, only said she was *willing* to . . . "You said, *If you must take a life*, Laura. So let's face it: God doesn't want you up there yet. Maman is out of danger now, and you are *not* going to die."

The doctor examined her thoroughly and gave her a sedative. But I couldn't sleep a wink.

So I stayed up and immediately honoured part of my promise. I laid on paper every last detail of what happened the night Maman almost died, lest I forget. Since then, I've been writing secretly every chance I get — I stay up at night a lot to do so, because there's just too much to do around the house during the day. I've tried to remember everything else about our family's past. The story starts when Papa met Maman at the big celebration party that ended the War in 1918. I've been wearing Grand-Papa out with endless questions. Other than that, I work from memory, asking Papa for a detail here and a piece of information there, without ever telling him what I am doing. Yesterday, I bought a beautiful notebook at the general store across the street and I take every free minute I have to transcribe the whole story in it, with my best pen and ink. I'll offer it to my family as a New Year's present. Bernard says he wants Maman and Papa to learn about his getting the call while they're reading the story, and not before. I hope my account accurately conveys that awesome moment.

Journal, what happened that night was very important, but part of it just can't be put into words — the incredible whirlwind that suddenly cast a new light on everything.

Maman is getting better and it's just wonderful. Was it the effect of the new medication? Or was it indeed a miracle? Well, perhaps the true miracle is that we are a happy family again, as close-knit as before, but now fully aware of how great a privilege it is to be so.

Mind you, Journal, Bernard-the-Pest still teases me every chance he gets, but — would you believe? — I just laugh it off.

Hattie has lived her whole life in Formosa, though her parents are Canadian. When her family moves back to Canada, there is so much to notice, and so much that is different from the small island where she grew up.

JEAN LITTLE *herself immigrated to Canada from Formosa (now called Taiwan) in 1939 when she was seven years old, just before World War II broke out. It was a sort of reverse immigration for a girl who "looked "Canadian but knew so little of life in Canada.*

Hattie's Home
～
The Diary of Hattie Middleton

Vancouver to Toronto
July – September 1939

Monday, July 31, 1939

This morning, Mother said how excited she was to be coming home to Canada. I said, "It's not MY home."

"Poor Hattie," Mother said. Then she went to the cabin and fetched this exercise book. She wants me to write a diary for one month about what it is like "coming home" to Canada. I said I would because I am sick of being stuck on this ship with nothing new to do.

Tuesday, August 1, 1939

I asked Mother how I should start and she said why not begin with a list of what makes Formosa feel like home.

So here goes.

Home is our missionary compound in Taipei. It has high walls and a big gate with flags above it, the Rising Sun for the Japanese and the Union Jack for the rest of us. I feel special when I walk through the gate, as though the compound belongs to me.

Home is our big house with its wide verandahs where we play.

Home is our Amah. She cried when we said good-bye. She came when I was a baby. I am ten now. She stayed to take care of Jonathan, who is eight, and then Will, who just turned three. Now Jon and I do lessons with Mother. In Canada, we'll go to regular school with other children.

Home is food too. In Canada, Daddy says they don't have mangoes and lichees and papayas. They don't eat with chopsticks. We don't eat with them all the time either, but we do whenever we have proper Chinese food.

It is time to go to the dining room for dinner but I will be back. This is interesting.

After Dinner

Will wanted rice pudding for dessert but when he found out it had no raisins in it, he cried. What a baby! Jon and I laughed at him and Daddy sent us away from the table.

Daddy keeps talking about war. I do not understand it. I asked Mother if we were in a war and she said no, but that Daddy is worried about the way things are going in Europe. I did not understand any better.

Home is water buffaloes and rickshaws and mountains and lilies growing wild and people pointing at us sometimes and saying things like, "Look at her big feet." We pretend we don't know what they are saying.

The boys just dragged me up on deck because, very

far away, you can see land. It has been a long time since we saw anything but the Pacific Ocean. Right now, the land is only a thin blue smudge far away. Sometimes a high wave hides it and then you see it again. Canada! I turned my back and caught Mother and Daddy gazing at it and grinning. They were holding hands! I felt left out.

Wednesday, August 2, 1939

The land looks real now. We will get there today. We will dock in Vancouver, and then go by train to Toronto. I asked if it was like Avonlea and Mother and Daddy laughed at me. Toronto is a big city, they say. Avonlea is a made-up village, not a real place.

Will I find a bosom friend like Diana Barry in Toronto? I have never had one. There were only a couple of boys my age in the compound, no girls.

No more lifeboat drills, thank goodness. I was scared they would lower me into a lifeboat and it would float away, leaving Mother behind.

I just thought of another thing. Home is chewing on a stalk of sugar cane. Mother says they chew gum in Canada.

After we get off this ship, we are staying overnight with friends of Daddy's. Then we will go on a train across Canada. We will stop in Regina to visit relations. Will they all want to kiss us? I don't like being kissed by people I don't know. I would rather shake hands or bow. I don't even know what to say first to Canadians. Do you say "How do you do?" or just "Hello" or "Good morning"? Saying "Hi" is rude.

I asked Daddy about this and he said any of those would be fine. There is not one right thing. I like the way it was in Taipei. There was one proper thing. Christians always said *"Pengan,"* which means "Peace." But there is no special greeting for church people in Canada.

Later

We had to pack everything up so we will be ready to go ashore. I hated shutting the trunk lid down on my dolls, Natasha and Emily. It was better when I laid them on their stomachs so they could not see it coming.

People kept stopping packing to check on Canada. The boys dance about and cheer. I am so glad my whole family is coming to Canada with me. I really do know they are the most important part of home.

Thursday, August 3, 1939

We are here in Vancouver at Daddy's friend's house. (It is much smaller than our house in Taipei.) We call them aunt and uncle even though they aren't.

When we got off the ship, Uncle Ralph grabbed my mother and swung her right off her feet. She laughed! Will and Jon thought it was funny but it made me want to pull her away. Is this how Canadians act?

His wife, Aunt Thelma, smiles with her lips shut. You never see her teeth. But her eyes are nice.

At lunch, she gave me plain bread and butter when I didn't want the salmon sandwiches she had ready. I love bread and butter. Mother was all excited because we were going to drink fresh milk. We hated it. Canned milk is so much better. Mother was disgusted with us.

After lunch, they took us to a park to play. It was strange seeing so many white people. I caught sight of one girl with bright red hair! Just like Anne Shirley.

The other thing that is amazing is hearing everybody talking English. I asked Mother if they didn't speak other languages here and she said some did, but here most people spoke English just as most people in Formosa spoke Chinese.

Friday, August 4, 1939

On the way home, we stopped at a drugstore and had ice-cream sodas. I never tasted anything so good. They put two scoops of ice cream in a big tall glass and then some syrup and then squirt on fizzy stuff, which fills up the glass. They give you a straw and a long-handled spoon so you can get the last drop of ice cream. Mine was strawberry. Yummy!

When we got home, Daddy and Uncle Ralph were listening to the news on their big radio again and talking about war coming. A lot of grown-ups say there might be a war, but lots of others, like Mother, say it won't ever happen. I don't think I have ever met a German. I must ask Daddy if he knows any.

Saturday, August 5, 1939

Being on the train was exciting at first but we soon got tired and too hot. Then Mother got out our paper fans from Formosa. Even the flower pictures on the back looked cool. Waving them cheered us up.

We are going to sleep on the train tonight in curtained-off berths. Each one has a little window. I plan to stay awake and watch the world passing by. I have never seen the night move that way. We've only ridden on trains in the daytime. It is hard to imagine it.

Sunday, August 6, 1939

I stayed awake a long time. I was right about it being amazing to watch the night moving past my window. It was my own window, which felt special. I saw farmhouses with one light on and big dark barns and little stations, and once I saw a wild animal running across a field. It might have been a fox. The stars in the prairie sky look bigger than usual and they make different shapes here in Canada.

Monday, August 7, 1939

Mother has started reading *Little Lord Fauntleroy* to us. Even Will likes it because it has good pictures. Cedric sounds like a sissy but he isn't. Jon said he would never call his mother "Dearest" and Mother pretended to be hurt.

I should think of something new for my list but I am

too hot and fidgety. Mother calls feeling twitchy "having the peasly-weaslys-and-the-jeejams." I don't know how to spell it.

Tuesday, August 8, 1939

The prairies just go on and on and on with nothing surprising. But at sunrise, the sky grows enormous and streaked with rose and gold. Daddy says it is breathtaking and he is right.

"Next stop Regina," the conductor is shouting. I can't write more.

Wednesday, August 9, 1939

Great-aunt Harriet calls me "Harriet darling." I like being called Hattie better but I don't say so. When Mother's parents died, Aunt Harriet took care of her and her brothers. Mother says she never made them feel like a burden. I do wish she didn't keep patting me on the top of my head.

The boys and I slept in the bedroom that was Mother's when she was my age. Aunt Harriet gave me a book which used to be Mother's. It is called *The Secret Garden* and is by the same writer who wrote *Little Lord Fauntleroy*. I am saving it until I have a room I don't have to share with little brothers.

Some cousins came after supper. They wanted us to say things in Chinese. Jon and Will did and the cousins laughed. When they went on pestering me, I said, "You are bad children," in Chinese. But I would not translate what I said. Mother laughed.

When Daddy got the grown-ups talking about Hitler, the cousins left. I am glad they don't live in Toronto.

Our train leaves very early tomorrow morning.

Thursday, August 10, 1939

Before we went to sleep last night, Daddy took us outside in our nightclothes and showed us how to find the Big Dipper. Jon and I saw it but I think Will just pretended. We will soon go through Winnipeg. I am too sleepy to write any more.

Much Later

I slept through Manitoba, most of it anyway. We are in Ontario at last but Daddy says we still have a long way to go. Canada is so much bigger than Formosa. It is wild here, with big rocks and little lakes and lots and lots of evergreen trees. The birds are different too.

We will get to Toronto tomorrow morning. We finished *Fauntleroy* and now we are going to start *Winnie the Pooh*. Piglet reminds me of Will. It is not a Canadian book. Daddy says he will find us one when we get to Toronto.

We have learned all the words to "O Canada" and "God Save the King" so we will be able to sing them when we start school. It is not our native land though.

Friday, August 11, 1939

Next stop Toronto. Daddy's sisters will meet the train. I must put my book away or I might lose it.

Saturday, August 12, 1939

We have three aunts and a grandmother in Toronto. They are Daddy's mother and his sisters. The aunts all came to meet us at Union Station. In Daddy's stories they are children, but they are not children now and it is hard to believe they ever were. They laugh a lot and they tease Daddy as if he were a little boy still. The station is like a palace. Maybe not quite. But so big and grand.

They took us home to their apartment and fed us. They showed us their balcony where they watched the King and Queen ride by when they were here in May.

"I sat right here and she waved to me," Grandma said.

"You should have stood at attention," Jon told her, as though he were a grown-up and she was just a little girl. Everybody laughed at him, everybody but Mother. She never makes fun of us in public.

They talked about war coming too and about the Quintuplets. Now Mother and Jon want me to come and play Chinese checkers with them.

Later

I lost.

I forgot to write about the Quints. The aunts gave us

some pictures of the Quintuplets. They call them "the Quints."

They are five girls all born at once, like twins or triplets. Aunt Rose showed us lots of pictures of them which she had pasted into a scrapbook. Imagine having four sisters who were all my age and looked like me and had the same birthday! It might be fun once in a while, but more often like a nightmare. How would you know who you were?

Sunday, August 13, 1939

We have moved into our new house. It is a rented half house on Bedford Rd. You can hear the people next door through the wall. But it is tall. There are four floors if you count the cellar. I have a little room of my own. It feels a bit lonely. I am used to sharing with Will.

There is no proper garden to this house, just a space they call the backyard. But there is a vacant lot just up the road with one great climbing tree.

Today was Sunday but it was not a day of rest.

Monday, August 14, 1939

We went to Eaton's to get school clothes. It was huge and filled with things I had never seen before. Part of it is a bookstore and all the books are in English! Daddy found us a Canadian one called *Beautiful Joe* and he also bought *Tarzan of the Apes* for the boys.

Tuesday, August 15, 1939

I am too busy these days to think about Formosa much. People come and go. There are horses in the street pulling delivery wagons. Jon takes them sugar cubes when he can get any.

I have started reading *The Secret Garden.* Mary Lennox is like me in lots of ways. She has to leave India and everything is different for her when she comes to England. I like the story a lot.

Wednesday, August 16, 1939

My doll Emily came all the way from Formosa safely and then that awful, horrible Will threw her out the window and her head is broken. I was teasing him, but that was not a good enough reason. Her eyes came out and I cannot stop crying.

Thursday, August 17, 1939

Aunt Margaret took Emily to The Doll Hospital. They say they can make her good as new. Then Aunt M. gave me a new doll. She is as big as a real baby and she has the loveliest smile and big blue eyes. If you push a place in her back, she says, "Ma-ma." She has pink clothes and white socks and shoes.

I am naming her Bella because that means "beautiful."

Friday, August 18, 1939

I am forgetting to write about what makes Canada different. Well, one thing is the streets. In Formosa there aren't sidewalks and stoplights. The road there is full of people in rickshaws, on carts, in cars, driving their water buffaloes, children playing, people carrying buckets on a yoke that sits on their shoulders. They carry water or vegetables sometimes. Once in a while, a sedan chair. People laugh and call out to each other and shriek at the children and make a lot more noise than Canadians. Canadians don't talk to strangers much, but in Formosa nobody is a stranger. Here people obey more rules and the houses all have numbers and sit in a row.

Bedtime

We are in bed but it is still light out. I don't see why we cannot stay up until it gets dark. It is like that poem "Bed in Summer" by Robert Louis Stevenson. He knew just how I feel.

When it gets dark, I still am homesick here, homesick for Taiwanese night sounds. We used to hear the lions in the zoo sometimes. And *geta* clacking along the streets. You don't see clogs like that in Canada. Or hear them. Toronto has some noise, but not so friendly.

Saturday, August 19, 1939

The people in the other half of our house are moving out. New people are coming.

Aunt Rose took us to Sunnyside, where we went swimming in a pool. There was a high slide that went down into the water and a big kid pushed Jon so that he fell from the top. He landed halfway down on a metal rod and scraped his back and then he slid off and fell to the ground. I was furious and I cried but Jon didn't. He just gritted his teeth and told me to stop making such a racket. I was feeling sorry for him one minute and wanting to murder him the next. Aunt Rose made us all come home and Mother put mercurochrome on his wounds.

Sunday, August 20, 1939

We were going to go to church this morning when Mother looked at Will. He was crying and he had stuff coming out of his ear and, when Daddy took his temperature, he had a high fever. "Poor Will," Mother said. "The shoemaker's child goes barefoot."

It means that Daddy, being a doctor, should have noticed Will's ear infection. Just like a shoemaker should see his child had no shoes.

Mother spent all day with him and left me and Daddy to get the meals. Jon was no help.

Monday, August 21, 1939

Aunt Rose has moved in with us and is helping Mother with the unpacking. Will is not all well but he is a little better.

After lunch, Mother is taking Jon and me over to

Jesse Ketchum School to arrange for Jon and me to get enrolled. I wonder if we will meet our teacher. I don't think so.

Later

It is a big school. Mother had to show our work from Formosa and prove we could do the lessons here. I saw a girl and boy who looked about our age, waiting with their father. I wanted to speak to them but it was not the right time.

I heard the father say, "Sit still, Elsie." I think that was her name. She was looking at us over her shoulder.

Tuesday, August 22, 1939

I can't sleep. I have decided to write about something that worries me in my Canada book. I don't quite understand this thing. This is it.

I feel strange here because we are not different. Always we have been special. People have stared at us and talked about us and laughed at the way we look. I thought I hated it. But it is queer — I miss it. I can't understand why it feels as though I am less interesting or something. I will think this over. I wonder if Jon feels it. If I asked, he would not admit it, I am positive. I feel ashamed almost.

Daddy says each human being is unique, one of a kind. But I feel much less unique in Toronto.

Wednesday, August 23, 1939

I visited Grandma today. It was sort of nice. Grandma tells the same story over and over. I wonder why she does not remember that she just told it.

When I came home, Will said he has learned a new Canadian song called "The Maple Leaf Forever." He says it has a wolf in it. Daddy laughed and told Will that Wolfe was a general, not an animal.

Thursday, August 24, 1939

The war, the war, the war. They call it THE war now, as though it has already started. Mother still says they will not be so stupid. Aunt Anne says Mother is too innocent for words. I asked what she meant but she would not explain. I am sure it was unkind.

Aunt Margaret took me out for an ice-cream soda, which was scrumptious. I had chocolate this time.

Friday, August 25, 1939

We went to the movies and saw Charlie Chaplin. People laughed their heads off but I felt sorry for him. We saw Hitler in the newsreels. How can anyone believe what he says? He seems crazy. I am very glad he is not here in Canada.

I think I am beginning to stop missing Formosa and sometimes feel more at home here. I worry about going to school though. I have always wanted to but now I am not so sure.

Saturday, August 26, 1939

Mother took us to Boys and Girls House, which is a library *filled* with children's books. I did not know there were so many books in English. I took out *The Story of the Treasure Seekers* and a fat book of fairy tales. In that library they are so nice and they think reading matters more than anything.

Beautiful Joe turned out to be terribly sad.

I finished *The Secret Garden* and I have started reading it over again. It is the best book I ever read.

Sunday, August 27, 1939

We went to Bloor Street United Church this morning. Mother stayed home with Aunt Rose, and Daddy and the boys and I went without them. This is the first time I have gone to church in Toronto. It was not the same as church in Formosa. For one thing, it was over much sooner. Then, when we said the Lord's Prayer, everyone except the minister mumbled. They didn't even say "Amen" out loud. They all shut their eyes and bowed their heads as though they were praying to their shoes. Even Daddy did, although I could at least hear him.

But even in church, they talked about war and they prayed for guidance and we sang "O God, our help in ages past." Jon and Will went down with the younger children but I shook my head and Daddy smiled and let me stay with him. When I got sleepy, he gave me a peppermint and a prescription pad and pencil so I could draw. I was glad to get home though and I read all afternoon.

Monday, August 28, 1939

The other side of our house is empty now. New people are moving in today or tomorrow. I am going to play outside all day so I can see them the moment they arrive.

Tuesday, August 29, 1939

Nobody moved in today. They were busy cleaning. But I was too shy to ask them any questions. Mother says she is sure the family will come tomorrow, although not until afternoon.

Wednesday, August 30, 1939

They came just before three. I could hardly believe my eyes. The girl is the one we saw in the office at Jesse Ketchum. Her name is Elsa, not Elsie. She is taller than I am and very thin. Her hair is as fair as mine. She has it hanging down in long braids. She wears glasses. She has a brother named Dirk who is Jon's age. They don't have little ones though. Mother baked bread and took them a loaf. She found out that their last name is Gunther.

Daddy went over after supper and I can hear the two men talking about war. What else?

Thursday, August 31, 1939

I thought of going over to say hello to Elsa but I felt too shy. I think she might feel shy too. Jonathan and

Will got Dirk to come with them to the vacant lot. Jon said No Girls Allowed. I didn't care. I hung around waiting for Elsa to come out. But I think they were still cleaning.

Jon says they are German but they are Canadian citizens. They came from Hamilton because her father lost his job. They aren't a bit like Hitler.

Our father is getting ready to start doctoring soon. He has a friend who wants a partner.

Friday, September 1, 1939

The Germans swept through Poland today. I think that is what Daddy said. I didn't ask what he meant exactly because I don't want to have to sit and be told. But it is bad and it is getting more and more like that War is coming.

I took chalk out to draw on the sidewalk and Elsa came out with coloured chalk. We did not say much but we had fun all the same. We made pictures of houses with white chalk and put in the details, like flowers, with coloured.

Daddy was over talking to Mr. Gunther again. They came here from Germany when he was a child. He is afraid of what is going to happen in Europe.

Just before Daddy came home, I heard the two of them burst out laughing, though. It was wonderful. It seems ages since I heard Daddy laugh.

Saturday, September 2, 1939

Elsa and I played dolls all morning and went to the vacant lot with the boys after lunch. We played Tarzan. Elsa got to be Jane but I did not mind because I got to be the animals. Jon said we had to have Mowgli in it too. Of course, he's from another book, but we gave in since he is such a great character.

Daddy would not come to supper with the rest of us because he is hunched up next to his big radio waiting for news from England. Mr. Gunther came over at nine o'clock to listen too.

Sunday, September 3, 1939

Daddy was right.

When I got up this morning, he was at the radio already even though it was early. Then he sent me up to get Mother. We all heard the prime minister in England declare war! Mother started to cry, although she was quiet about it. The aunts came. We thought of staying home from church but Mother said today we need to pray. So we went. We sang "Onward, Christian Soldiers" for the children's hymn. Some people cried. It does not feel real.

After

I am supposed to be asleep.

I can write by the streetlight outside. Daddy was right about war coming, but I want to say that Mother was right too when she said it would be stupid. I feel very muddled up.

But one thing I know now. I will stand on guard for Canada if I can figure out how.

Monday, September 4, 1939
Labour Day

School starts tomorrow. Elsa and the boys and I spent most of the day in the vacant lot, which we have named The Greenwood. We did not talk about the War or school starting. When we came home, the four of us arranged to meet in the morning. If our mothers come to the school with us, we will go together so that, when they have to leave, we will still have each other.

Tuesday, September 5, 1939

I only have one page left, but that is fine because there are only two moments I want to remember.

The first moment is when we had finished singing "God Save the King."

"Remain standing, class, while we sing 'O Canada,'" Miss Murdoch said. Elsa and I are in the same class. We sit right across the aisle from each other. We had talked about this and we looked at each other and smiled when we came to "our home and native land." Canada is not my native land. I was born in Formosa. Elsa's parents are Canadian citizens but she was born in New York while they were visiting her aunt and uncle. We sang the words anyway. We are different enough. But I was glad she was there.

The rest of the day was long. We came home for lunch at noon but we had to go back.

Then, when the afternoon ended and we came down our road, Will was waiting on the front steps. When he saw me coming, he jumped up and ran to the door yelling, "Hattie's home! Hattie's home!"

And I was.

About the Authors

LILLIAN BORAKS-NEMETZ is a Warsaw ghetto survivor who spent some of the war years hiding in Polish villages under an assumed name. She is the author of several Holocaust-related novels: *The Old Brown Suitcase* (winner of the Sheila A. Egoff Award), *Ghost Children*, *The Sunflower Diary* and *The Lenski File*. She is co-editor of an anthology of writing about the Holocaust: *Tapestry of Hope: Holocaust Writing for Young People*. Lillian has written an adult novel featuring the character in *The Old Brown Suitcase*, fourteen-year-old Slava Lenski, about how a grown woman attempts to cope with wounds suffered from an unresolved childhood trauma.

MARIE-ANDRÉE CLERMONT is a Quebec writer and translator. After writing suspense and adventure stories, she devised the Faubourg St-Rock series of novels for teens, a daring concept in which the day-to-day problems of adolescents are addressed openly. Her own works in Faubourg St-Rock include *L'engrenage*, *La marque rouge* and *La gitane*. Parts of her story in *Hoping for Home* — Bernard's "hearing the call," Laura's willingness to give her life to save her mother's, and the mine disaster that killed seven men — are inspired by actual events she heard about while growing up.

DR. AFUA COOPER is a scholar and poet, and the author of *My Name Is Phillis Wheatley* and *My Name Is Henry Bibb*, as well as the Governor-General's Award nominee *The Hanging of Angélique: The Untold Story of Canadian Slavery and the Burning of Old Montréal*. Afua's doctoral studies focused on Black communities in Ontario in the nineteenth century, particularly on anti-slavery crusader Henry Bibb. She is also the author of several books of poetry, most recently *Copper Woman and Other Poems*.

BRIAN DOYLE is the award-winning author of dozens of YA novels, among them *Boy O'Boy; Pure Spring; Angel Square; Hey, Dad!; Uncle Ronald; Up to Low; You Can Pick Me Up at Peggy's Cove* and the Spud Sweetgrass novels. Many of his stories are set in and around the Ottawa Valley in the decades after World War II, a time when young people were wondering if the atomic bomb was going to end their world before they could grow up. Brian, raised with tall tales spun around the kitchen table, writes with an ear for diction and rhythm, and champions stories that unfold for the reader in subtle ways.

RUKHSANA KHAN has written novels such as *Wanting Mor*, based on the story of a girl in Afghanistan, and *Dahling, If You Luv Me, Would You Please, Please Smile*, about a teenage Muslim girl managing to find a way to stand up for her own traditions. Her picture books include *King of the Skies* and *The Roses in My Carpets*.

Rukhsana's collection of eight stories, *Muslim Child*, depicts Muslims living in different parts of the world. Her latest picture book, *Big Red Lollipop*, describes the difficulties of fitting in to a new culture. Rukhsana grew up in a small southern Ontario town where she and her family were the only Pakistani Muslims.

JEAN LITTLE is a member of the Order of Canada, and the author of nearly fifty novels and picture books, among them *Orphan at My Door*, *Brothers Far from Home*, *If I Die Before I Wake*, *Exiles from the War*, *Dancing Through the Snow*, *From Anna* and *Mama's Going to Buy You a Mockingbird*. She is the daughter of medical missionaries. Jean's story for this anthology is based on her own arrival in Canada from Formosa (now known as Taiwan), as a "Canadian" girl who knew little of life in Canada, just before World War II broke out.

KIT PEARSON is the award-winning author of many children's novels, among them *Whispers of War*, *The Daring Game*, *A Handful of Time*, *Awake and Dreaming* and *A Perfect Gentle Knight*. Her Guests of War Trilogy (*The Sky Is Falling*, *Looking at the Moon*, *The Lights Go On Again*) about children from England who spend the war years in Canada, has become a Canadian classic. Kit's mother and aunt attended The Bishop Strachan School; Kit was able to use some of her aunt's letters from this era while researching her story. Her newest novel is *The Whole Truth*.

RUBY SLIPPERJACK is a professor in the Department of Indigenous Learning at Lakehead University, and the author of half a dozen novels, among them *Honour the Sun*, *Silent Words*, *Little Voice* and *Dog Tracks*. Ruby grew up on her father's trapline on Whitewater Lake, until she moved to attend a residential school in Sault Ste. Marie. Apart from teaching and writing, she tries to spend as much time as she can "out in the bush," close to the traditional way of life of her family. These traditions provide much of the fabric of her stories.

SHELLEY TANAKA's award-winning non-fiction titles include *On Board the Titanic*, *Attack on Pearl Harbor* and *Amelia Earhart: The Legend of the Lost Aviator*. Her books have won the Silver Birch Award, the Science in Society Children's Book Award, the Information Book Award and the Orbis Pictus Award. She is also a highly respected editor who has worked with Canada's finest children's writers, including Martha Brooks, Brian Doyle, Deborah Ellis, Sarah Ellis, Tim Wynne-Jones, Rukhsana Khan, Jean Little and Paul Yee. Shelley teaches in the MFA program at Vermont College. Her mother's family was interned in Kaslo during World War II.

IRENE N. WATTS is the award-winning author of a trilogy about the Kindertransport program (*Good-bye Marianne*, *Remember Me* and *Finding Sophie*), as well as two books about Home Children (*Flower* and *When the Bough Breaks*). Her most recent novel, *No Moon*, features a young nanny aboard the *Titanic*. Irene co-edited the anthology *Tapestry of Hope: Holocaust Writing for Young People*. She herself escaped from Europe just prior to World War II as one of the ten thousand children rescued via the *Kindertransport* program, which helped get Jewish children out of Europe before the onset of the war.

PAUL YEE has written many award-winning picture books and novels, contemporary and historical, about the Chinese experience in Canada, most notably *Ghost Train, Roses Sing on New Snow, Tales from Gold Mountain, The Bone Collector's Son* and *The Curses of Third Uncle*. His non-fiction book is *Saltwater City: An Illustrated History of the Chinese in Vancouver*. Paul's most recent book is *Blood and Iron*, the story of a young Chinese boy helping build the Canadian Pacific Railway, in the I Am Canada series. His play about British Columbia's Chinese coal miners, *Jade in the Coal*, premiered in Vancouver in 2010. Paul was born in Saskatchewan, and was raised in Vancouver's Chinatown by his aunt.

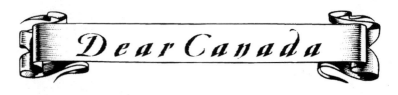

No Safe Harbour, The Halifax Explosion Diary
of Charlotte Blackburn by Julie Lawson

Not a Nickel to Spare, The Great Depression Diary
of Sally Cohen by Perry Nodelman

An Ocean Apart, The Gold Mountain Diary
of Chin Mei-ling by Gillian Chan

Orphan at My Door, The Home Child Diary of Victoria Cope
by Jean Little

A Prairie as Wide as the Sea, The Immigrant Diary
of Ivy Weatherall by Sarah Ellis

Prisoners in the Promised Land, The Ukrainian Internment Diary
of Anya Soloniuk by Marsha Forchuk Skrypuch

A Rebel's Daughter, The 1837 Rebellion Diary
of Arabella Stevenson by Janet Lunn

A Ribbon of Shining Steel, The Railway Diary of Kate Cameron
by Julie Lawson

A Season for Miracles, Twelve Tales of Christmas

To Stand On My Own, The Polio Epidemic Diary
of Noreen Robertson by Barbara Haworth-Attard

A Trail of Broken Dreams, The Gold Rush Diary
of Harriet Palmer by Barbara Haworth-Attard

Turned Away, The World War II Diary
of Devorah Bernstein by Carol Matas

Where the River Takes Me, The Hudson's Bay Company Diary
of Jenna Sinclair by Julie Lawson

Whispers of War, The War of 1812 Diary of Susanna Merritt
by Kit Pearson

Winter of Peril, The Newfoundland Diary
of Sophie Loveridge by Jan Andrews

With Nothing But Our Courage, The Loyalist Diary
of Mary MacDonald by Karleen Bradford

Go to www.scholastic.ca/dearcanada for information on the Dear Canada series
— see inside the books, read an excerpt or a review, post a review, and more.